D1192193

You're going
to be great,
Angel Face!
xoxo Mom

Double
Trouble
forever!
—Flynn

Copyright © 2021 by Netflix. JULIE AND THE PHANTOMS:™/© NETFLIX, INC. All Rights Reserved.

All rights reserved. Published by Scholastic Inc., *Publishers since 1920* SCHOLASTIC and associated logos are trademarks and/or registered trademarks of Scholastic Inc.

The publisher does not have any control over and does not assume any responsibility for author or third-party websites or their content.

No part of this publication may be reproduced, stored in a retrieval system, or transmitted in any form or by any means, electronic, mechanical, photocopying, recording, or otherwise, without written permission of the publisher. For information regarding permission, write to Scholastic Inc., Attention: Permissions Department, 557 Broadway, New York, NY 10012.

This book is a work of fiction. Names, characters, places, and incidents are either the product of the author's imagination or are used fictitiously, and any resemblance to actual persons, living or dead, business establishments, events, or locales is entirely coincidental.

ISBN 978-1-338-73115-6

10 9 8 7 6 5 4 3 2 1   21 22 23 24 25
Printed in China   62
First printing 2021
Book design by Lizzy Yoder with Tim Palin Creative

Stock photos ©: 26 label and throughout: APCortizasJr/Getty Images; 27 stamp and throughout: Aquir/Getty Images; 27 folder and throughout: axstokes/Getty Images; 124 bottom: Chase Olivieri/EPA/Shutterstock. All other stock photos © Shutterstock.com.

NE NIGHT
ONLY!
Sunset
Curve
TICKETS SOLD OUT
LIVE AT THE
ORPHEUM

HOLLYWO

TRA

"Sunset Curve fans are heartbroken."

Three more of Hollywood's rising stars have been tragically snuffed out too soon. Members of the rock band Sunset Curve died last weekend just hours before their sold-out performance at the Orpheum. Lead singer and guitarist Luke Patterson, bassist Reggie Peters, and drummer Alex Mercer, all age 17, succumbed to a deadly case of food poisoning from eating hot dogs sold by street vendor Sam 'N' Ella's Dogs. The surviving band member, rhythm guitarist Bobby Shaw, declined to comment.

While the band wasn't a household name—yet—there's

OD GEDY

Sunset Curve

Lone surviving band member, Bobby Shaw

a good chance you've heard one of their can't-get-it-out-of-your-head indie hits. Their shows were an unstoppable burst of energy, and this band was well on their way to stardom.

Sunset Curve fans are heartbroken, several of them having met the band members just hours before their deaths. Many became followers not only for Sunset Curve's music, but also because Luke, Reggie, and Alex "were just nice guys," one fan told us. "They never hesitated to share their love of music with everyone."

Life is short, so the next time you drive into the sunset, we hope you shout out the lyrics of your favorite Sunset Curve song in their memory . . .

"NOW OR NEVER"

Take off
Last stop
Count down 'til we blast open the top

Face-first
Full charge
Electric hammer to the heart

Clocks move forward
But we don't get older, no
Kept on climbing
'Til our stars collided

And all the times we fell behind
Were just the keys to paradise

Don't look down
'Cause we're still rising
Up right now
And even if we
Hit the ground
We'll still fly
Keep dreaming like we'll live forever
But live it like it's now or never!

Hear the noise
In my head
It's calling out like a voice I can't forget

One life
No regrets
Catch up, got no time to catch my breath

Clocks move faster
'Cause it's all we're after now
Won't stop climbing
'Cause this is our time, yeah
When all the days felt black and white
Those were the best shades of my life

Don't look down
'Cause we're still rising
Up right now
And even if we
Hit the ground
We'll still fly
Keep dreaming like we'll live forever
But live it like it's now or never!

We ain't searching for tomorrow
'Cause we got all we need today

Living on a feeling that's been running through our veins

We're the revolution that's been singing in the rain

Don't look down
'Cause we're still rising
Up right now
And even if we
Hit the ground
We'll still fly
Keep dreaming like we'll live forever
But live it like it's now or never!

It's now or never!

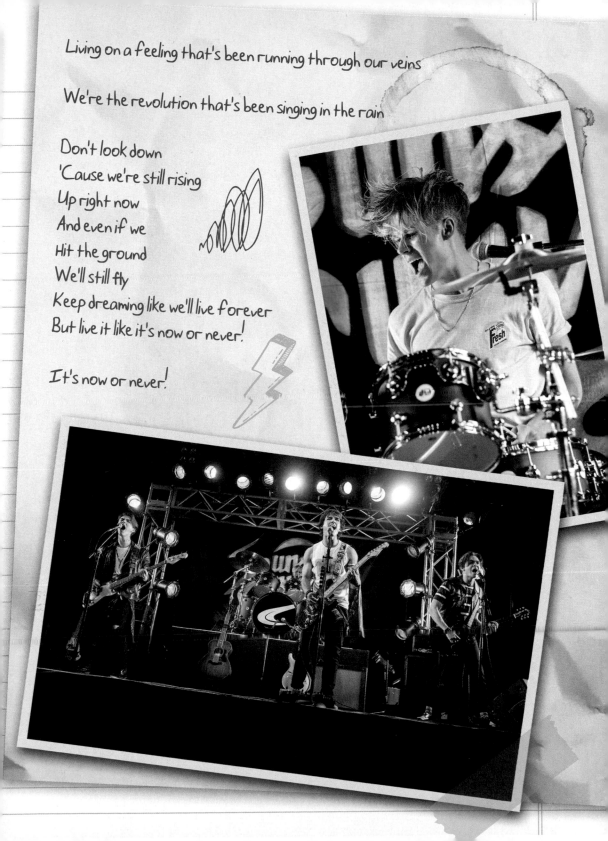

This is it. Today is my last chance to keep my spot in the music program. Mrs. Harrison said that I can keep avoiding it—the piano, performing, whatever—and I understand. I really do! But ever since Mom died, I haven't been able to write a single note.

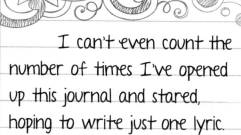

I can't even count the number of times I've opened up this journal and stared, hoping to write just one lyric.

Flynn's been awesome and sent me a bunch of playlists to inspire me. Dad and Carlos cooked some weird recipes that they said would help "bring out my inner creative energy." (The only thing it brought out was a stomachache—and not the "butterflies before a performance" kind.)

It's just that . . . every time I try to write something or when I look at a piano, I just freeze up. And then I think of Mom, and it's like losing her all over again. I can't find that connection to music anymore. It's gone—just like Mom.

Maybe it's for the best that I leave the music program.
I don't even know <u>what</u> I like anymore. And I know it would
definitely make Carrie happy. She's had it out for me for a while.
And I bet Nick wouldn't even notice if I was gone.

Do I really want that, though? This music program meant
everything to me. And Mom was so proud of me when I got in . . .

But there's just no music in me anymore.

Welcome to Los Feliz PERFORMING ARTS High School, Bobcats!

Your journey toward greatness begins now. The Los Feliz music program is one of the most prestigious and sought-after programs in Hollywood. And we've got the alumni to prove it! These very halls are where some of today's biggest and most talented stars got their start.

We here at Los Feliz High embrace everyone's journey to discover their identity. Whether it's music, art, fashion, or even *sports*, we encourage you all to become the best that you can be.

You've beat out the competition to get here—so take advantage of this opportunity! Let's hear that Bobcat ROAR!

LOS FELIZ
BOBCATS

My dad, Ray, is the kind of person who sees life like a photograph. Every moment he captures is precious and worth protecting. He has an eye for detail and a HUGE heart. He's always looking out for me and Carlos to make sure we're okay.

His job as a photographer means he has the weirdest hours. He's either working in the middle of the day or at night, so it can be hard for him to keep track of the little things in life. Like his keys, his meals, and even his own head sometimes!

But he never misses a single baseball game for Carlos, and he's always there for me when I need a shoulder to lean on and someone to talk to. He will always do what's best for his family, even if it means selling the house that we grew up in if it will help us heal.

I know Dad misses Mom just as much as we do, but he tries not to show it. I wish he'd let us comfort him once in a while.

My brother, Carlos, is the kind of person who takes everything day by day—except for when it comes to his weird obsession for the paranormal. He binges on <u>Ghost Hunters</u> and is convinced our neighbor is actually a lizard person.

Sometimes I think this is his way of feeling closer to Mom, like he thinks her ghost is watching over us or something.

Ghosts or no ghosts, my little brother always knows how to make me laugh, and he's always there for me in his own, weird way.

Wow, Dad, these photos are great!

They really stir up some great memories, don't they? Remember when your mom decorated every inch of the house for Christmas? Even my underwear were Christmas themed!

Remember when Flynn and I volunteered to make cupcakes for the spirit rally and the frosting exploded? Our kitchen was blue for a whole week!

The only thing I remember is trying to clean the inside of the fridge. How did frosting get there anyway?

I still find blue stains in random places.

HOM sweet HOME

Sometimes I go out into the garage and part of me still expects your mom to be in there playing the piano or watering her plants.

Me too.

What are you going to do with all the instruments in there, Dad?

We could probably sell them and make a little extra cash.

Don't you think it's weird there was so much stuff in the loft when you and Mom moved in? I wonder where it all came from . . .

ANGEL CITY
REAL ESTATE

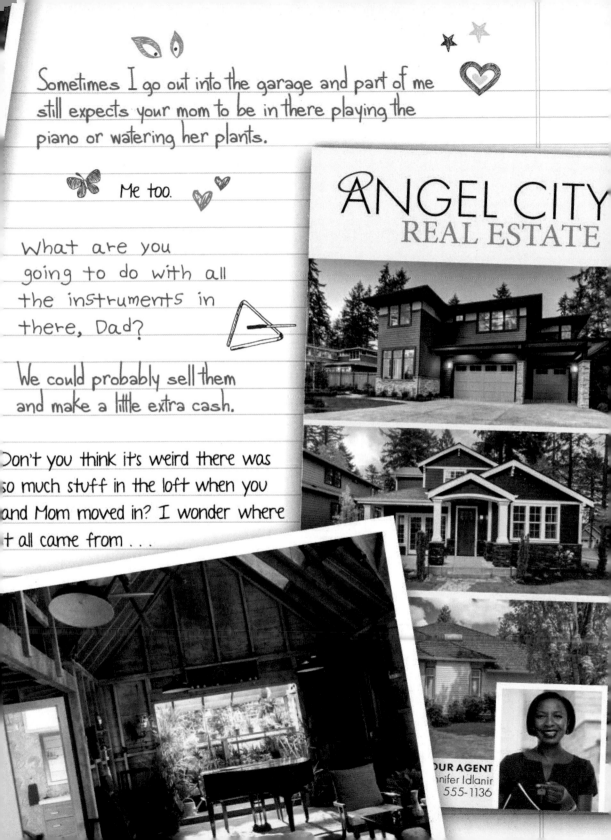

OUR AGENT
nnifer Idlanir
555-1136

"Wake Up"

Here's the one thing
I want you to know
You got someplace to go
Life's a test, yes
But you go toe to toe
You don't give up, no, you grow

And you use your pain
'Cause it makes you you
Though I wish
I could hold you through it

I know it's not the same
You got livin' to do
And I just want you to do it

So get up, get out, relight that spark
You know the rest by heart

Wake up wake up if it's all you do
Look out, look inside of you
It's not what you lost
It's what you'll gain
Raising your voice to the rain

Wake up your dream and make it true
Look out, look inside of you
It's not what you lost
Relight that spark
Time to come out of the dark

Wake up
Wake up

Better wake those demons
Just look them in the eye
No reason not to try

Life can be a mess
I won't let it cloud my mind
I'll let my fingers fly

And I use the pain
'Cause it's part of me
And I'm ready to power through it

Gonna find the strength
Find the melody
'Cause you showed me how to do it

Get up, get out, relight that spark
You know the rest by heart

Wake up wake up if its all you do
Look out, look inside of you
Its not what you lost
Its what you'll gain
Raising your voice to the rain

Wake up your dream and make it true
Look out, look inside of you
Its not what you lost
Relight that spark
Time to come out of the dark

Wake up
Wake up

So wake that spirit spirit
I wanna hear it hear it

No need to fear it you're not alone
You're gonna find your way home

Wake up wake up if its all you do
Look out, look inside of you
Its not what you lost
Its what you'll gain
Raising your voice to the rain

Wake up your dream and make it true
Look out, look inside of you
When you're feelin' lost
Relight that spark
Time to come out of the dark

Wake up
Wake up

I swear that I'm not crazy, but I somehow accidentally summoned a boy band in the garage!

Excuse me? A BOY BAND?!

Yeah! We don't do choreography! We rock!

They never let me dance onstage...

OKAY? ALSO, BOUNDARIES! STOP READING MY JOURNAL!

So you DO think we're cute?

BOUNDARIES!

Dad asked me to clean up Mom's studio. There was all this old stuff in the loft, and I found this demo CD there. But when I played it, POOF! Three cute teenage ghosts just appeared out of nowhere! ☺

They introduced themselves and said they were in a band called Sunset Curve. They died in 1995 from ... street dogs? (I honestly don't want the details.)

I thought I was crazy, but the ghosts were just as freaked out as I was. Not to mention, even though no one can see them but me, everyone can <u>hear</u> their music. So weird.

I felt bad kicking them out of the studio. They didn't do anything wrong, and it's not like there's some ghost hotel they could go to. (Or is there?) But they promised to keep the volume down when they're playing music and not talk to me around my family.

I've had a pretty rough day, but I can't even imagine how it must feel to suddenly realize you've been dead for more than twenty years—and you can't eat anymore. Maybe I should leave the fridge door open for them, just so they can see what they're missing . . .

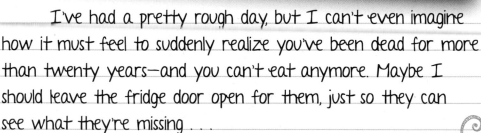

"This Band Is Back"

Can you, 'a can you hear me?
Loud and clear
We gotta get, we gotta get ready
'Cause it's been years

1, 2, 3, 4!

Ooh, ooh, this band is back
Ooh, ooh, this band is back

Whoo, whooo
Whoo, whooo
Whoo, whooo

Can you, yes we can, can you hear me?
Loud and clear!
We gotta get, wanna get, we gotta get ready
'Cause it's been years!

Ooh, ooh, this band is back
Ooh, ooh, this band is back

Whoo, whooo
Whoo, whooo
Whoo, whooo
Whoo, whooo

It's been a few days since Luke, Reggie, and Alex dropped into my mom's studio, and I've never met a band made up of people who are so different yet still so in sync.

Take Luke, for instance. He loves music more than anyone I know. It's like he breathes it. And he knows he's talented (although that makes him a little overconfident at times). He's the kind of person who always gets what he wants, because he just GOES for it.

But the lyrics he writes and the messages behind his songs show that he's actually a sweet guy who just loves what he does. And that's what steals the show.

Alex is the only one who can keep the other guys in check. He and I actually have a lot in common, like how we get really overwhelmed sometimes and just want to run away. He's so easy to talk to. With everything that's happened to him, I think he really appreciates having someone he can vent to about how to deal with all these changes.

Then there's Reggie. He's definitely the weirdest of the three, but I think that's part of his charm. And it turns out that he's a HUGE nerd. He loves Star Wars, and he even knows how to play D&D! (He made me swear not to say anything, though.) He's also strangely attached to my dad. He says they're "kindred spirits."

Reggie tries to see the best in every situation. Sometimes it doesn't work out, but he never loses faith. I think that's awesome.

These totally different guys somehow complement each other so well. It's like they were born to be a band. They're lucky they found each other, and I'm lucky they found me.

REPORT: **00248769441**

OPERATIVE: **C. MOLINA**

C L A S S I F I E D

Mission: ███████████████████████

Objective: ███████████████████████

Carlos's Ghost Log #1

I thought my sister was crazy when she said the garage was haunted, but lately there have been some weird things going on around the house.

Every time I come home from school, the fridge is open. And I keep hearing music playing in the garage, but as soon as I go to check it out, the music stops. At first I thought it was just Dad being Dad, until I saw the floating orbs in the pictures.

These pictures are proof that our house is haunted! Floating orbs are, like, ghost hunting 101!

But who is it? Is it Mom? Is it some vengeful spirit? And why are they hanging out in the garage? I should look into this more.

I guess I'll have to do some research by rewatching every season of <u>Ghost Hunters</u> again.

YOU GOT THE SPIRIT?

WE GOT THE

BOBCATS

Join us this Friday afternoon for the **Los Feliz Spirit Rally**

SPECIAL PERFORMANCE BY DIRTY CANDI!

The Bobca

Los Feliz High School Student Newspaper

JULIE STEALS THE SPOTLIGHT!

JULIE MOLINA stole the show—and her top spo back in the music program!—during last week's spirit rally. It' been over a year since the Los Feliz musical prodigy faded into the background of the school's talented student body. And recently,

Claw Times

Volume 10, Issue 13

rumor had it that she had even lost her spot in the program altogether.

After this latest performance, though, there's no doubt that those rumors are false! Headliner Dirty Candi was quickly overshadowed by Julie's impromptu concert, beginning with a quiet piano solo before wowing the crowd with a complete band who appeared onstage out of thin air!

We caught up with Julie right after and asked her how she pulled off this impressive comeback performance.

The answer: holograms.

Technology isn't just for auto-tune and electric backtracks anymore. Looks like Julie is back with a whole new beat!

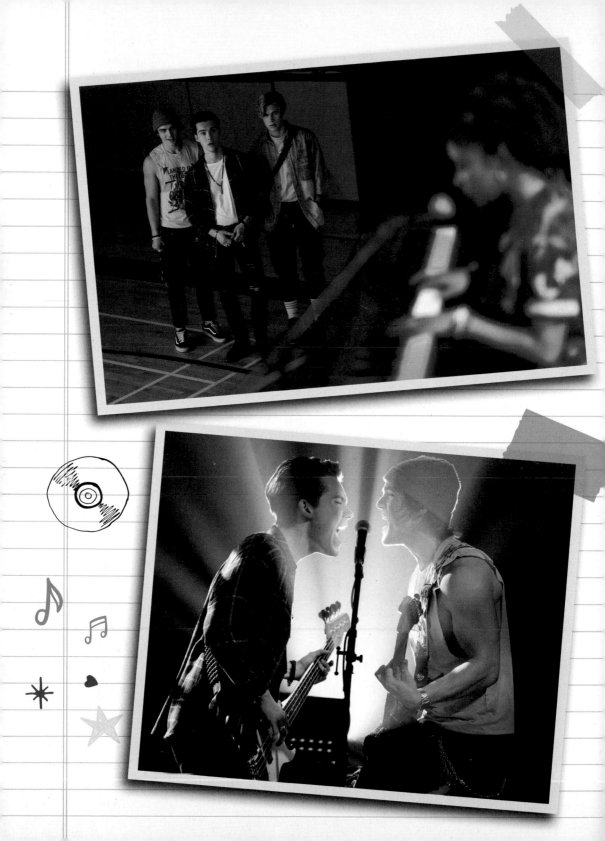

That was one of the craziest things we've ever done. I can't believe how much I missed playing for a crowd!

Definitely beats that one time we played at an all-you-can-eat buffet.

Dude . . . you're missing the point. They didn't just hear us—they SAW us!

And they LOVED us. Julie killed it. And she got her spot back in the program!

I still can't believe you actually gave one of your songs to Julie. I thought you said those songs were Sunset Curve exclusives.

I made an exception. She's got the pipes and the talent. She just needed the right song to win them over. Plus, we kind of owe her for letting us stay in the studio.

Sure, that's the ONLY reason.

It's still a little crazy that the crowd could see us when we played with Julie.

Yeah, but why? What's the reason for that?

The power of friendship?

Yeah, bro. Definitely the power of friendship.

This is still freaking me out. These are a lot of changes to deal with all at once. Being dead . . . people hearing us . . . now people can see us when we play with Julie?!

Dude, it's gonna be fine. Less nervousness, more excitement. We have another chance at making it big again!

I hope Julie told those cheerleaders I'm single.

And dead?

Not that part!

"Bright"

Sometimes I think I'm falling down
I wanna cry I'm callin' out
For one more try
To feel alive
And when I feel lost and alone
I know that I can make it home
Fight through the dark
And find the spark

Life is a risk but I will take it
Close my eyes and jump
Together I think that
we can make it
Come on let's run and—

Rise through the night you and I
We will fight to shine together
Bright forever and
Rise through the night you and I
We will fight to shine together
Bright forever

And times that I doubted myself
I felt like I needed some help
Stuck in my head
With nothing left

I feel something around me now
So unclear lifting me out
I found the ground I'm marching on

Life is a risk but we will take it
Close my eyes and jump
Together I think that we can make
Come on let's run and—

Rise through the night you and I
We will fight to shine together
Bright forever
And rise through the night you an
We will fight to shine together
Bright forever

The times that I doubted myse
I felt like I needed some help
Stuck in my head

With nothing left

And when I feel lost and alone
I know that I can make it home
Fight through the dark, and find the spark

And rise through the night you and I
We will fight to shine together
Bright forever
And rise through the night you and I
We will fight to shine together
Bright forever

My best friend, Flynn, is the kind of person who doesn't just walk to the beat of her own drum—she remixes it and then blows the crowd away. She's one of the most confident people I've ever met, and she's not afraid to push her way through the crowd. Everything she does, from her music down to her earrings, is meant to showcase her unique talent.

She never doubts herself, and that confidence is contagious. Because she wants other people to shine WITH her. She doesn't tolerate anyone who tries to steal the spotlight all for themselves (aka Carrie).

Double Trouble forever!

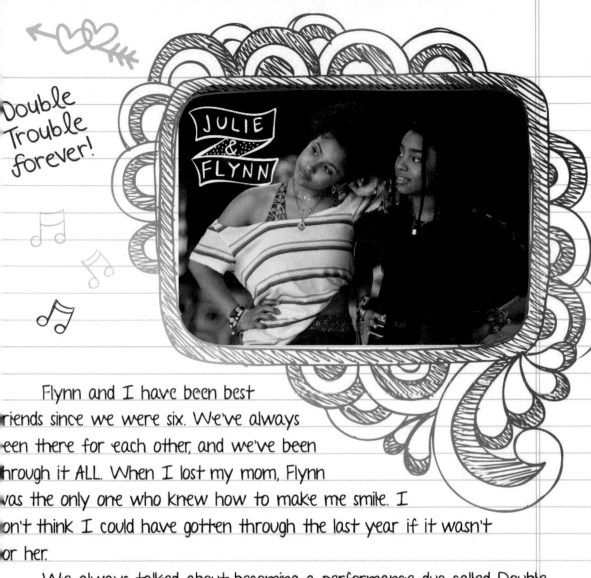

JULIE & FLYNN

Flynn and I have been best friends since we were six. We've always been there for each other, and we've been through it ALL. When I lost my mom, Flynn was the only one who knew how to make me smile. I don't think I could have gotten through the last year if it wasn't for her.

We always talked about becoming a performance duo called Double Trouble (her name, not mine)—playing a blend of rock and hip-hop. But now that I've joined the guys, Flynn decided to become Julie and the Phantoms' manager instead. She's already created accounts for the band on all the major social media platforms, and she's been trying to book us gigs anywhere she can. I'm so lucky to have her in my corner.

Word of advice? When it comes to friends, always find the ones who want you to shine.

FLYNN'S CODE TO CONFIDENCE

- Confidence doesn't just come from within, it comes from outside, too. Whenever I wear an outfit that screams "Me!" it boosts me up and makes me feel like I can take on the world.

- Whenever you get a case of imposter syndrome, remember that positive always beats negative! If your head tells you that you don't deserve something, make a list of all the reasons you DO. Because trust me, you're probably more qualified than you think.

- Remember that the spotlight doesn't belong to just one person. If the world is a stage, every role is important. So give credit where credit is due. If it's your friend's chance to shine, lift them up! Your time will come.

- Do what makes you happy. You'll never be truly confident until you love what you do AND who you are.

Fantasmas/Ghosts

Fantasmas existen
ellos murmuran sus canciones
al viento
para que los
escuchen

Ghosts exist
They whisper their music
to the wind
so you can hear
them

"Flying Solo"

If I leave you on a bad note
Leave you on a sad note
Guess that means I'm buying lunch
that day

I know all your secrets
You know all my deep dish
Guess that means some things they
never, they never

Change
We both know what I, what I,
what I
Mean
When I look at you it's like I'm
looking at me

My life, my life would be real low,
zero, flying solo
My life, my life would be real low,
zero, flying solo without you

Hey
Yeah-e-yeah
Hey
Yeah-e-yeah

My life, my life would be real low
zero, flying solo without you

Yeah, you know who I'm likin'
Way before I liked them
Duh . . .
'Cause you liked them first

And if somebody hurts you
I'm gonna get hurt, too
That's just how we work, yeah,
that's just how we work
It will never

Change
We both know what I, what I
what I
Mean
When I look at you it's like I'm
looking at me

My life, my life would be real low
zero, flying solo
My life, my life would be real low
zero, flying solo without you

Hey
Yeah-e-yeah
Hey
Yeah-e-yeah

My life, my life would be real low, zero, flying solo without you

My life, my life would be real low, zero, flying solo
My life, my life would be real low, zero, flying solo without you

Hey
Yeah-e-yeah
Hey
Yeah-e-yeah

My life, my life would be real low, zero, flying solo without you

I started liking Nick after I heard him play a rock ballad version of one of Trevor Wilson's first hits. A cute guy who also loves Trevor Wilson? And who can play it, too? My heart was stolen the minute he hit that high note.

Nick is a sweetheart, and he's naturally talented at everything he does. He's even great at <u>sports</u> (well, great for Los Feliz High, anyway). And somehow he gets along with everyone, even Carrie . . .

I just don't get it! What does he see in Carrie, anyway? I mean, sure, she's talented, and she does work hard—even if she uses her dad's name and money to get everything she wants—but she's just so . . . mean! And Nick is so nice! And cute. And has a great smile.

But the point is, Nick is too good for her. And he barely knows I exist! I'm just that weird girl who sometimes dances down the hall and accidentally steals people's drumsticks.

I'm just saying, "Julie's Hologram Band" doesn't have that wow factor, you know what I mean?

What should our band name be, then?

I don't know. What was their original band name?

Sunset Curve.

Ugh, too '90s grunge. It needs to be something fresh, catchy, easy to hashtag.

They don't even know
what a hashtag is.

WOW, they have a lot to catch up on.

I know, right? It took me an hour to
explain what YouTube is.

Maybe we can play around with their ghostiness.

I'm not sure . . . wouldn't that be risky?

Girl, no! It'd be like an inside joke that no one else gets. Like One Direction. Where are they going? No one knows. Julie and the Spirits? Julie and the Ghostly Band?

Stop.

Julie's Cuties?

Please stop.

Julie and the Friendly Ghosts?

I'm BEGGING you to stop.

The Phantom of the Garage?

Julie's Phantoms?

You know what? I don't totally
hate that last one.

I'll think about it some more during French. Au Revoir!

REPORT: **002487694**

OPERATIVE: **C. MOLIN**

TOP SECRET

C L A S S I F I E D

Mission: ██████████████████

Objective: ██████████████████

Carlos's Ghost Log #5

Okay, so after I watched <u>Ghost Hunters</u> for the twelfth time, I made a list of ways to ward off the ghosts that are haunting the house. Plus, I asked Dad what other remedies Abuelita used to use when something ghosty was going on. So here's what I have so far:

- Salt—not just for seasoning anymore! If you make a circle with salt and stand inside it, ghosts can't touch you.
- I downloaded a <u>Ghost Hunters</u> app that helps identify ghosts with your camera (sort of like how Dad captured the orbs in the garage).
- Dad said Abuelita used to just yell at ghosts to get out of her house. Should I try that? A good backup plan anyway.
- Dad also said that Abuelita used Vicks for everything . . . I don't think that would work for a ghost unless it had a cold though. (Can ghosts get sick? Something to research . . .)
- Find out what their unfinished business is and solve it for them.

Ever since I first performed with the guys at the spirit rally, I've felt like I'm back to my old self again. I feel so light, it's like I'm basically floating through school. All the music I thought I'd lost is running through my veins, making it impossible to keep still. I'm either tapping or humming or dancing my way down the halls. Flynn said she was happy to see me back to my weird self again, and I couldn't even get mad at her because I'm happy, too!

It's all thanks to Luke, Reggie, and Alex. If it wasn't for them pushing me to perform, I don't know what would've happened to me. I might have lost my music for good.

And what's even more incredible is how EASY it is to perform with them. All the fear and anxiety I used to have, the preperformance jitters, they disappear as soon as the guys start playing with me. Making music with them feels as easy as breathing.

I can't help but think my mom sent them to me—that she had a hand in bringing them to my life the exact moment I needed them the most. The guys said they haven't met her, but who's to say? I'm in a band with ghosts, so anything's possible.

List of Potentials Gigs for Julie and the Phantoms

- Los Feliz High school dance ← *I'm DJing, so I have an in there.*

- Marta's cousin's sister's daughter has a quinceañera in a month

- Los Feliz High monthly book club ← *Next month's book is <u>Dealing in Dreams</u> by Lilliam Rivera—it's postapocalyptic, and rock music will totally set the mood!*

- Singing in the Caffeine

- Soothing Smoothies

- Eats and Beats Café ← *I've heard they do a regular open mic night. Hard to get on the list, though?*

- Rockin' Coffee Beans

- Keepin' It Cheesy

- Next fall's homecoming dance?

- Prom? *Technically, we can't go yet, but maybe underclassmen can still perform?*

Julie
and her
HOLOGRAM
BAND

Tonight
at the Dance!
9:00 p.m.

DJing
by Flynn

I didn't realize how much I missed music until I literally spent an entire weekend with Luke writing one song after the other. My hand kept cramping up, but there were so many things I wanted to put down on paper that I couldn't stop.

I do feel a little bad, though. I barely texted Flynn at all, and I haven't spent as much time with my family. But I think they understand. They know how happy I've been, throwing myself back into something I haven't done in over a year. Sometimes I even catch Dad humming a song I've practiced with the guys. Alex doesn't think Dad counts as a "fan" because he's family, but it still makes me smile.

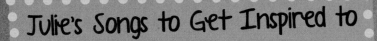

Julie's Songs to Get Inspired to

"My Future" by Billie Eilish

"Contra Todo" by iLe

"cardigan" by Taylor Swift

"El Loco" by Misa 'E Gallo

"Una Flor" by Émina

"Vámono" by Buscabulla

"Adore You" by Harry Styles

"Crooked Teeth" by Trevor Wilson

"Formation" by Beyoncé

"Killer Queen" by Queen

"Para Darte" by Los Rumberos & Los Rivera Destino

"She Looks So Perfect" by 5 Seconds of Summer

"Lost" by Frank Ocean

"You Broke Me First" by Tate McRae

"Supalonely" by BENEE ft. Gus Dapperton

"Un Dia (One Day)" by J. Balvin, Dua Lipa,
and Bad Bunny

"POV" by Ariana Grande

"Someone You Loved" by Lewis Capaldi

"I Got the Music"

Ain't gonna fight it 'cause it's useless
I can't get this music out of my head

It's like the beat is taking over
Weight off of my shoulders,
dancing instead

And something's feeling different
in the hallways
Something's looking, looking like
it's changed
I've been moving to the rhythm
for the whole day
A million lyrics running through
my brain

Everybody here we go, this
thing is unstoppable
Haven't felt this in a minute,
it's incredible

I got the music
Back inside of me
Every melody and chord
Can't stop the music
Back inside my soul
And it's stronger than before

I got the music
It won't let me go
I got the music
Just like a radio
I got the music
Streaming from my soul
And it's stronger than before

Don't care if everybody's watchin'
Silence ain't an option
It's out of my hands

I feel the beat takin' me higher
Baby this is fire. This is my jam

And something's feeling different
in the hallways
Something's looking, looking
like it's changed
I've been moving to the rhythm
for the whole day
A million lyrics running through my brain

Everybody here we go, this
thing is unstoppable
Haven't felt this in a minute,
it's incredible

I got the music
Back inside of me
Every melody and chord
Can't stop the music
Back inside my soul
And it's stronger than before

I got the music, it won't let me go
I got the music, just like a radio
I got the music, streaming from my soul
And it's stronger than before

Can you hear it?
Can you hear the music?
I got the music back inside of me

Can you hear it? Can you hear the music?
I got the music back inside of me

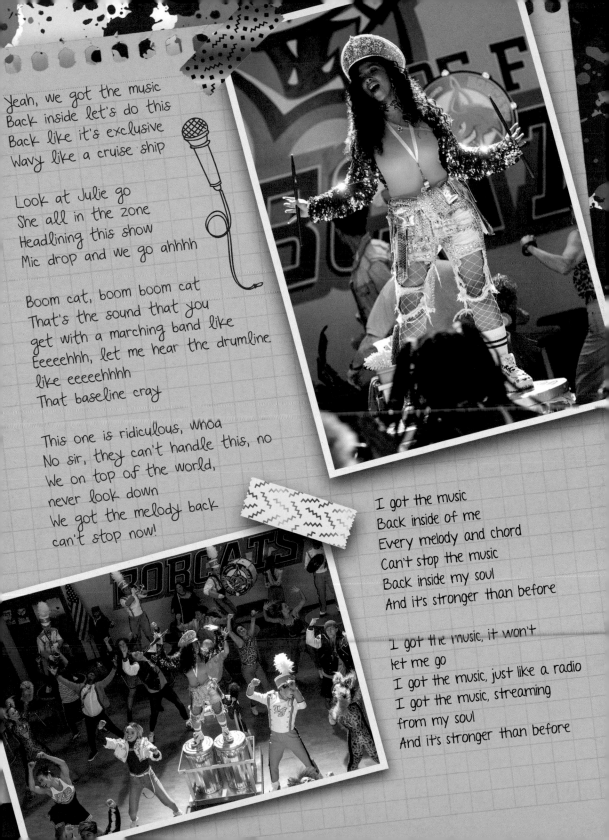

Yeah, we got the music
Back inside let's do this
Back like it's exclusive
Wavy like a cruise ship

Look at Julie go
She all in the zone
Headlining this show
Mic drop and we go ahhhh

Boom cat, boom boom cat
That's the sound that you
get with a marching band like
Eeeeehhh, let me hear the drumline.
like eeeeehhhh
That baseline cray

This one is ridiculous, whoa
No sir, they can't handle this, no
We on top of the world,
never look down
We got the melody back
can't stop now!

I got the music
Back inside of me
Every melody and chord
Can't stop the music
Back inside my soul
And it's stronger than before

I got the music, it won't
let me go
I got the music, just like a radio
I got the music, streaming
from my soul
And it's stronger than before

REPORT: 002487694443
OPERATIVE: C. MOLINA

CLASSIFIED

Mission: ███████████████████

Objective: ██████████████████████

Carlos's Ghost Log #8

Okay, now it's getting personal. The ghosts touched my laptop! And played music on it! I know it was them because it's not even stuff I would listen to—just a bunch of old rock bands.

At first I thought it was Julie, but she and I have a strict agreement to never touch each other's stuff after the Tamagotchi incident (RIP Mr. Snuffies). Then I thought it was Dad, but he doesn't know my password.

There can only be one explanation: the studio ghosts! I guess this confirms my theory that they're <u>not</u> tied to the studio. If they can walk around freely, that would explain my computer— and why I keep finding the fridge door open.

I need to figure this out. Mom listened to a lot of rock music, too. What if one of the ghosts really <u>is</u> her? And if she's been coming in the house, what if she knows that I don't change the toilet paper roll when it runs out? Or that I broke a side of that expensive vase when I practiced baseball inside and turned it around so no one would notice? Or that I hid pasteles under my bed?

But if the ghost <u>isn't</u> Mom . . . I have to protect my family. I'm the only one who knows the truth about what's going on!

SUNSET CURVE-ING INTO THE SPOTLIGHT

Learn more about Luke Patterson, Reggie Peters, Alex Mercer, and Bobby Shaw from LA's hottest up-and-coming rock band, Sunset Curve—plus, their plans for what comes next!

INTERVIEWER: With a summer tour just around the corner, it feels like this is the year for your big break. Feeling nervous? Excited?

LUKE: All of it. I can't wait to start the tour with the band and share our music with more people.

INTERVIEWER: Looks like you guys already have fans just waiting to see you play, too, based on the sold-out shows.

ALEX: It's awesome that we have so many people who love and connect to our music. We want to reach out to as many listeners as possible.

INTERVIEWER: Any people in particular you want to give a shout-out to? Or a special someone any of you boys want your music to reach?

REGGIE: Oh! Sandy from Sandy's Patties—you make the best burgers!

ALEX (TO REGGIE): I don't think that's what they meant.

LUKE: The person I want my music to reach the most will know it when they hear it.

INTERVIEWER: Speaking of reaching out, I have a few questions from the fans. A few quick-fire questions. First one: Cats or dogs?

LUKE, ALEX, AND BOBBY: Dogs

REGGIE: Hamsters!

INTERVIEWER: Haunted fridge or haunted bathroom?

LUKE: What? This is a fan question?

BOBBY: There are no such things as ghosts.

INTERVIEWER: Pizza or tacos?

REGGIE: Burgers.

ALEX (TO REGGIE): I don't think you understand this game.

INTERVIEWER: Last question: Where do you see yourself in twenty-five years?

LUKE: In the Rock and Roll Hall of Fame.

BOBBY: With a helicopter!

SET LIST
ORPHEUM THEATRE

"MY NAME IS LUKE"

"GET LOST"

"BRIGHT"

"LONG WEEKEND"

"CROOKED TEETH"

"NOW OR NEVER"

"ENCORE"

Trevor Wilson broke into the music industry like a speeding bullet in the mid-nineties, an overnight success with a debut album that broke several records. His music has inspired so many of today's rising stars—several of whom have dedicated their own success to Trevor.

But how does a teenage LA native beat the odds and become a star? Find out in this exclusive interview!

Interviewer: *Let's start from the beginning, with your first album. What inspired you to write such profound lyrics?*

Trevor: When I was seventeen, that was when I felt I was the most myself. Playing music on the streets, at the beach, during book clubs—anywhere I could. And when I was playing unnoticed, that's when my lyrics were at their purest, untouched and flowing out of me like water over a smooth stone.

Interviewer: *Do you think you and your music have evolved throughout the years?*

Trevor: Like life, everything must change. And as my life changed, so did my music.

Interviewer: *Do you have any words of wisdom to share with aspiring musicians?*

Trevor: Always carry good karma, and stay true to your spirit.

What is he even talking about? He couldn't even rhyme two words together.

He evolved into a substitute teacher.

Trust me. Your karma is right here, and it's going to bite back.

I just can't stop thinking about it. LUKE wrote all those songs I love? Not my idol, Trevor Wilson—the one who inspired me to be a singer-songwriter? His lyrics changed my life!

Well, I guess <u>Luke's</u> lyrics changed my life.

I can't wrap my head around this. Why would Trevor steal Luke's lyrics? Weren't they friends? (By the way, Bobby? Really?) That's like me stealing Flynn's designs—the ultimate betrayal. Our friendship would be over for good.

I'm really worried about the guys, too. Finding out that someone they trusted stole everything they worked for and took all the glory really hurt them. Luke took it the hardest. And I can understand. Those were HIS songs, HIS lyrics, with someone else's name on them. Luke said it wasn't about the money; it's the fact that their friend backstabbed them and basically erased them from memory—as if they never existed.

And I get it. I do! But I also know how important it is to
let go of the past. What's done is done, and they can't change what
happened. Plus, they're in a new band now, with new music. The best
revenge, in my eyes, is to prove how much better they are without
their "friend."

I left them alone to cool off, and I needed the space, too. It
was a lot to take in. But I have to go back to make sure they're
not going to do something crazy, like haunt Trevor Wilson's mansion.
They wouldn't go that far, right?

Right?

IDEAS FOR HAUNTING BOBBY TREVOR

All my years watching horror movies are about to pay off.

I wouldn't exactly call <u>Casper</u> a horror movie.

It has ghosts in it! It counts!

Focus!

Right! Vengeance. Revenge. The last laugh. I say we throw his underwear into the pool.

That's cute. But I don't think that screams "haunting."
Maybe we can mess with the stuff around his house? You know, lights flickering, floorboards creaking, the classics.

Sure, but we have to make sure he knows it's US. That we know what he did. We need to shake him up a little.

Oh! How about we go into his dreams and make him relive that one time someone hit him in the face with a burger and it had extra mayo on it. Or, we could steal his helicopter and crash it into the ocean.

I love the enthusiasm, Reggie, I do. But let's take a different approach. Alex, that friend of yours, do you think he has more tricks up his sleeve?

Oh! Oh! Like giving a ghost wedgie.

I'm sure Willie can help us out. (And no, not with wedgies.)

HELLOOOO
BOBBY

I think I lost count of how many slices of pizza I ate after number twenty.

I never thought I'd actually get to eat a meatball sub while hanging on a chandelier. This place really does make dreams come true.

I never want to hear about dreams ever again.

Can we come back here every night?

I mean we could! Being able to actually talk to Lifers and eat food—PLUS good music? It's like an amusement park but everything is free.

That Caleb guy is a little creepy, though. He smiles too much.

Relax, man. That's showbiz for you!

Did you guys see where Willie got off to by any chance? I lost him after dancing with Dante and Fuego.

No, sorry. I was a little distracted.

"Other Side of Hollywood"

Let me introduce myself
We got some time to kill
Consider me the pearly gates to your new favorite thrills

We could go make history, or you could rest in peace
But here there ain't no misery
'Cause on the other side we live like kings

Whatcha gonna do?
Whatcha gonna do?
Oh
Letcha body loose
Letcha body loose

Whatcha gonna do?
Whatcha gonna do?
Oh
Show you a thing or two
'Cause you ain't seen nothing

Life is good
On the other side of Hollywood

Life is good
On the other side of Hollywood

So welcome to the brotherhood
Where you won't be misunderstood

Life is good
On the other side of Hollywood

Everything has got a price
But happiness is free

Just so happens
You're in luck
We've got a vacancy

We can set the night on fire
And break out of the scene
Your soul print on the Walk of Fame
On the boulevard of your wildest dreams

Whatcha gonna do?
Whatcha gonna do?

Boys

Letcha body loose
Letcha body loose

Whatcha gonna do?
Whatcha gonna do?

Boys

It ain't bragging if it's true
Now you ain't seen nothing

Life is good
On the other side of Hollywood

Life is good
On the other side of Hollywood

So welcome to the brotherhood
Where you won't be misunderstood

On the other side of Hollywood

The rain don't blind the rising souls
They got too much to see

I got your glamour, got your gold
Got all you'll ever need

Let me hear you now

The rain don't blind the rising souls
They got too much to see

I got your glamour, got your gold
Got all you'll ever need

Watch me make a move
Watch me make a move

Boys

I said
Watch me make a move
No, I don't disappoint

AMEN
Watch me make a move
I'm ya number one choice

Watch me make a move
Come on and give me that noise

A tomb with a view
Ain't it something

Life is good
On the other side of Hollywood
Life is good
On the other side of Hollywood

So welcome to the brotherhood
Where you won't be misunderstood
Life is good
On the other side of Hollywood

So welcome to the brotherhood
Where you won't be misunderstood
Life is good
On the other side of Hollywood

Ain't it the best
Long live the dead

Los Feliz High School Student Newspaper

GHOSTED BY THE PHANTOMS

LAST NIGHT'S dance ended on a sad note after Julie Molina's band, Julie and the Phantoms, was unable to perform due to technical malfunctions. The band was a last-minute addition to the roster. They were set to join the dance's original—and, as it turned out, only—entertainment, Flynn Taylor, who DJed.

Claw Times

Volume 10, Issue 14

Partygoers were disappointed by the hologram band's cancellation, as they hoped for a repeat of their mind-blowing debut performance at the recent spirit rally. (When asked why she didn't perform solo after her connectivity issues, Julie declined to comment.)

"I wanted to feel like I was at Coachella again. Instead, I felt like I was at my grandma's polka lesson," said one disappointed student.

"It started off with a bang and ended like a sad trumpet," another attendant said.

Luckily, the evening was saved by an after-party at student Carrie Wilson's beachside mansion. But will Julie and the Phantoms rise again?

Flynn would kill me if she ever read this, but she and Carrie actually have a lot in common. They're both confident, smart, and sassy, and they know what they deserve and how to get it.

The biggest difference is that one of them steals the spotlight while the other shares it.

Carrie and I . . . we used to be close. Once upon a time, we were, like, best friends. We had sleepovers at her mansion all the time, practiced together, even choreographed! But then things got complicated.

Suddenly, the Carrie I knew changed. She formed her girl group Dirty Candi, and started using her dad's money to pay for the same songwriters, choreographers, and designers used by famous pop singers. I barely even recognized her. And she started using every opportunity to flaunt that power wherever she went.

Suddenly, Dirty Candi was everywhere. Spirit rallies, dances, homecoming. She'd post a new YouTube video every other day, and she had a HUGE following on social media. She. Was. Everywhere.

And the thing is, Dirty Candi is actually really good. Their songs are catchy and make you want to dance. They're so good, but Carrie is still so MEAN.

And then! She started dating Nick! Who is a sweetheart!

I just don't get it! What does he see in her? I mean, yes, she's pretty and talented, but she's so rude to everyone (especially me). I just wish I could understand why she changed.

THINGS WE CAN DO AS GHOSTS

It takes a lot of energy, and sometimes whatever we're holding slips through our fingers.

Willie really helped us learn how to master this.

Oh my god, Alex, do you have a CRUSH? Shut up.

- ◎ **Hold things**

- ◎ **Summon our instruments**

- ◎ **Write things down**

- ◎ **Perform—but people can only hear us when we're on our own, and they can only see us when we play with Julie**

- ◎ **Prank hipsters in cafés while they're taking pictures of their food**

- ◎ **Go to whatever concerts or movies we want for free**

  We can sit wherever we want, too!

- ◎ **Instant travel = no more LA traffic!**

THINGS WE CAN'T DO AS GHOSTS

Truly tragic

◎ **Eat (unless we're at the HGC)**

Good thing we can talk to Julie still, huh, Luke? ☺

◎ **Talk with our fans**

◎ **Crowd surf**

Julie doesn't know how good she has it.

◎ **Perform our barbershop trio to get some cash**

Reggie, we don't need money if we're dead.

◎ **Photo shoots**

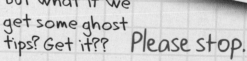

But what if we get some ghost tips? Get it?? Please stop.

◎ **Have a pet**

Not a dog or a kitten, or even a hamster!

◎ **Hang out with Ray**

Reggie, stop trying to be friends with Julie's dad.

But we have so much in common!

Our last trip with Mom was a couple of summers ago, to visit family in Puerto Rico. We drove all over the island, seeing the tourist hot spots like Viejo San Juan in the north and then going all the way down south, where we saw the bioluminescent bay in Parguera.

Dad always told us that the way Puerto Ricans speak Spanish is unique, and it's true! My cousins speak SO fast, and everything they say sounds like a melody, each sentence a song. Their dialect is a blend of English and Spanish, and they switch from one to the other without thinking twice.

And the food! So much food. From vendors who park on the expressway selling quenepas and empanadillas, to kiosks by the beach that fry bacalaítos and make alcapurrias. And then there was my abuelita Zoraida's homemade arroz con gandules y bistec encebollado. Everything we ate was mouthwatering, the flavors something that can't be imitated anywhere else. We drove two hours up a mountain just to go to a street that's dedicated to roasting pig. But my favorite meal in the entire trip was mofongo, fried plantains filled with meat or seafood. I still drool when I think about it.

Despite the hardships, the hurricanes, the earthquakes, and the bad times, Puerto Ricans are people who won't go down without a fight and who won't hesitate to add their own flavor into every-thing they do—be it food, protesting, or music. Even the way they speak is influenced by their history.

The culture in Puerto Rico is, at heart, about celebrating life. I hope one day we can go back again as a family. I think Mom would like that.

DAILY planner

WEDNESDAY

- Finish English project—a rendition of Shakespeare's Much Ado About Nothing as if it were written in 2020

- Math quiz

- French test

How this will help me become a musician, I don't know.

Ugh, I can't math today.

- Performing with Mrs. Harrison

- Lunch with Flynn—brainstorm ideas for social media and upcoming gigs

Make sure Dad remembers to drop him off after school!

- Baseball practice for Carlos

- Clean the kitchen / living room

- Homework

More math, ugh

- Audition with the guys

- Meditate before bed

Don't forget the "projector"!

Luke's Songs to Jam to

"My Sharona" by the Knack
"You Really Got Me" by the Kinks
"Say It Ain't So" by Weezer
Smells Like Teen Spirit" by Nirvana
"Voodoo Child" by Jimi Hendrix
"Little Girl Blue" by Janis Joplin
"Let's Dance" by David Bowie
"Sweet Child O' Mine"
by Guns N' Roses
"Learn to Fly" by Foo Fighters
"Good Riddance
(Time of Your Life)"
by Green Day

You gotta listen to
these songs, too! -J
"Do I Wanna Know?"
by Arctic Monkeys
"Youngblood"
by 5 Seconds of Summer
"Monster"
by All Time Low ft.
Demi Lovato and blackbear
"Loner"
by Maggie Lindemann
"High Hopes"
by Panic! At The Disco

C L A S S I F I E D

Mission: ████████████████

Objective: ████████████████████

Carlos's Ghost Log #12

I recently tried yelling at the ghosts—you know, to communicate with them. But it turns out that only got me grounded for waking up the neighbors.

So it was time for plan B. I decided to try using salt to protect the house, so the ghosts couldn't get inside anymore. In this one YouTube video I watched, the ghost hunters used salt to create a protective barrier while they talked to Moody McBungersome, an angry ghost who liked throwing newspapers at people and died after yelling at kids for too long.

So I sprinkled salt all over the house, especially in Mom's studio. Julie and Flynn have been hanging out there more and more often, and I have to be sure that nothing tries to hurt them.

UPDATE: I got grounded again. Dad said the floor feels crunchy, so now I have to vacuum the whole house.

My tia lives just around the corner from us, so she's been a frequent presence in our house for as long as I can remember. And by "frequent" I mean constant.

Tia is here every birthday, every holiday, every lost tooth, EVERY DAY. She always has the latest gossip from her Pilates class, and these days, she never visits without at least several days' worth of food (which is always delicious, thank you, Tia!).

And while Tia likes to get her nose in everyone's business, I know it comes from a good place. If it weren't for her, I think this house would've been a disaster zone ever since my mom—her own sister—died. If Tia hadn't been here picking up the pieces of our family, I don't know where we'd all be.

And sure, Tía doesn't really understand my love for music and why my program at school is so important to me, but I think that's just her way of trying to protect me from the real world.

One thing's for sure, she always serves up the best hugs. And arroz con pollo.

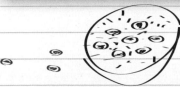

EATS & BEATS CAFÉ

OPEN MIC NIGHT

TONIGHT'S FINAL LINEUP

MUDDY ELECTRO

CUBIC INCHWORM

CONTACT INSANITY

PUDDLE OF LOVE

MAMMOTH HAMMOCK

TOXIC WASTELORD

ARTICHOKE

DIRTY CANDI

JULIE AND THE PHAT ONES

I just . . . I just don't get it. How do you make milk out of oats?!

Dude, we're not having this conversation again. Let it go.

You know what I don't get? Hipsters. What are they? Hippies of the 21st century? Why did Julie call my shirt "hipster material"? It's just a shirt!

And why do they take so many pictures of avocados? And why is coffee so expensive? Do they charge you by how many times you take pictures of it? $6 for a latte? It used to be $2!

I am not a hipster.

Two people just left this café wearing the same shirt you're wearing right now. I think you gave birth to hipsters.

I hate this place.

Oops!

"We're Sorry"

We're sorry!

So sorry!

~~Really Sorry!~~

How many sorrys do we need?
Five max.

~~Like really sorry~~

Should we make a remix and put it in her phone?

Remember the Dream Box episode? I don't think she'd appreciate us touching her phone.

We're super-duper

crazy stupid

sorry!

Luke! Why are you here? You almost gave me a heart attack!

You should be thanking me. You were yawning so loud your jaw cracked.

Why. Are. You. Here?

Right! Rehearsal! We should have rehearsal right after school.

Okay! Is it cool if Flynn comes?

As long as she stops poking my arm. It tingles.

I'll be sure to warn her. Now go ghost somewhere else.
I have to concentrate.

Also lyrics. I think I came up with a
few good ones for "Finally Free."
I'd love to read them if they
weren't in your messed-up
handwriting. It's like two
chickens got into a fight on
top of your notebook.
Julie, come on!
Poof away, chicken scratch.
We'll talk lyrics later.

Dad once told me that resentment is like a weed. It chokes up your feelings until all you have left are the bad ones. That's why it's so important to let go and find peace within yourself.

And, logically, I know I should've sat down and talked to the guys from the beginning. But every time I saw them, I relived standing alone on that stage, humiliated by Carrie, and so angry at myself for trusting someone again. I never thought being ghosted by ghosts would suck as much as it did.

It felt like the only thing they cared about was being famous and getting back at Trevor for stealing their music. And I do get it. If Carrie stole my music and got all the credit, I'd be furious. And, even though it all went down twenty-five years ago, to them, it feels like it just happened. That hurts.

But if Luke, Reggie, and Alex keep holding on to something that's in the past, they might never move on. And we almost lost something good because of it—our band.

We all had things to let go of. So we talked it out. And I learned why the guys—and especially Luke—felt so hurt. Their music wasn't just to get famous; it was their way of reaching out to the people who wouldn't listen to them.

We all agreed that what Trevor—no, Bobby—did is unforgivable. But ditching me was wrong, too.

It'll take time, and a lot of talking, but I think we're on our way to getting the band back and better than before.

"Finally Free"

Hearts on fire
We're no liars
So we say what we wanna say
I'm awakened
No more faking
So we push all our fears away

Don't know if I'll make it 'cause I'm falling under
Close my eyes and feel my chest beating like thunder

I wanna fly
Come alive
Watch me shine

I got a spark in me
Hands up if you can see
And you're a part of me
Hands up if you're with me
Now 'til eternity
Hands up if you believe
Been so long and now we're
finally free

We're all bright now
What a sight now
Coming out like we're fireworks

Marching on proud
Turn it up loud
'Cause now we know what
we're worth

We know we can make it
We're not falling down under
Close my eyes and feel my chest
Beating like thunder

I wanna fly
Come alive
Watch me shine

I got a spark in me
Hands up if you can see
And you're a part of me
Hands up if you're with me
Now 'til eternity
Hands up if you believe
Been so long and now
we're finally free
(2x)

I got a spark in me
And you're a part of me
Now 'til eternity
Been so long and now we're finally free

I got a spark in me
Hands up if you can see
And you're a part of me
Hands up if you're with me
Now 'til eternity
Hands up if you believe
Been so long and now we're finally free

Been so long and now we're finally free

So, I'm totally grounded because I snuck out (which is wrong), but I can't be upset because Julie and the Phantoms killed it at open mic night! It almost makes being grounded worth it. Almost . . .

Anyway, the show! Amazing. Standing ovations all around. People felt our energy and ate it up, and Carrie (who performed right before us) hated every minute of it. I still get goose bumps thinking about it.

The craziest part is that a music manager actually gave me her business card! I almost fainted right there!

Of course that's exactly when I got busted by Dad for sneaking out. I thought he was gonna pull the cord on the band for sure, but we had a long talk when we got home. After I explained to him that it was the guys who got me back into music, he understood how important the band is to me. But he set some ground rules: school first, then the band. It was an easy deal to agree to.

Andi Parker
Music Manager

Emai...
AParker©DestinyM...
Phone: 5...

Destiny Management

Let's talk—
invite
your dad!
—A

    I forget sometimes how important it is to talk to my dad about what's going on. Even if he doesn't really understand, he always listens and gives me a chance to express myself. If I was just honest with him about the band from the beginning, I wouldn't have had to sneak out in the first place.

    Lesson learned. Now I need to sleep. Today was a whirlwind, and I'm about to crash from the high of an awesome performance.

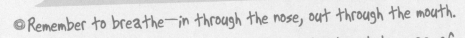

◎ Remember to breathe—in through the nose, out through the mouth.

◎ When I feel really tense, I dance it out. Shout-out to years of dance classes!

◎ Any kind of moving helps me loosen up. Drumming, walking—anything that makes me break a sweat clears my head and pulls me out of those anxious thoughts.

◎ It seems obvious, but talking to the guys or Julie always helps. They usually know exactly how to pick apart the things that are muddling up my head.

◎ Sometimes my anxiety makes my brain feel like it's filled with white noise, and even music won't help. I try to find an open space like the beach and just lie down and ride out the emotions. It's all temporary.

◎ The latest trick, apparently, is to just scream. I might have to try that more, now that most people can't hear me!

"Home Is Where My Horse Is"

I never needed a roof over my head
A soft pillow or a warm bed
No place to rest my weary heart
But as long as I'm riding
Into the curve of the sunset
There is no better home
Than where it's just me, my banjo
And my horse

Home is where my horse is
No walls can hold us back
Or the wild mountain roads
With the wind behind my back
I broke a few hearts who asked me
To stay there by their side
But my horse and I
Don't need a home
As long as together we ride

Hanging out with Willie is like riding a bike down a hill without breaks. The wind rushes over my face, I'm out of control, my blood's pumping as I go faster and faster—until I crash and burn.

This time, I'm crashing hard and fast. Willie is always moving, always running with no destination in mind. And I'm always chasing him, because I want to feel that rush that I only get with him.

I met him at exactly the right moment. Those first few times we hung out, when he taught me about being a ghost and got me out of my own head for a bit, were amazing. But lately, Willie hasn't been around as much. And every time I see him, he makes some excuse and runs away. I thought we had something—something REAL—but now he's avoiding me.

Ever since he took us to meet Caleb at the Hollywood Ghost Club, Willie hasn't been the same. I know it could just be my anxiety talking, but it really feels like he's acting guilty or hiding something from me.

I want to talk to him, and help him if I can, just like he helped me. But I can't do that if he keeps running away.

ALL EYES ON ME

Whenever I walk in the room
All the focus on me
The way I talk the way I move
They all want on my team

Not tryin' to brag, brag
But I'm flawless
I'm taking over your playlist
Ain't perfect but I can't miss, yeah
The party don't start 'til I walk in
I'm stealing all the attention
Don't get me started on mentions, yeah

Some might say I sound conceited
They don't get the shine that I get
Some get jealous
They can't help it
They wish they were me

I keep the party going all night, all night
I set the trends that you all like, all like
I make an entrance when I don't try, don't try
'Cause all I see is all eyes on me

I only lead I never follow, follow
I never open 'cause it's my show, my show
Don't know if people think I'm shallow, shallo
But all I see is
All eyes on me

They know my face
They know my name
Reputation on lock
It's not my fault I got the fame
Ain't my fault it won't stop
Yeah

I keep the party going all night, all night
I set the trends that you all like, all like
I make an entrance when I don't try, don't try
'Cause all I see is all eyes on me

I only lead I never follow, follow
I never open 'cause it's my show, my show
Don't know if people think I'm shallow,
shallow
But all I see is all eyes on me

When I grow up I wanna be me, be me
I'm my own goals just talking honestly
Must have won the lottery
ain't no one as hot as me
Stealing looks it's robbery
Everywhere I go
all eyes on me

Not tryin' to brag, brag
But I'm flawless
I'm taking over your playlist
ain't perfect but I can't miss, yeah

The party don't start 'til I walk in
I'm stealing all the attention
Don't get me started on mentions, yeah

I keep the party going all night, all night
I set the trends that you all like, all like
I make an entrance when I don't try, don't try
'Cause all I see is all eyes on me

Some might say I sound conceited
They don't get the shine that I get
Some get jealous
They can't help it
They wish they were me

I only lead I never follow, follow
I never open 'cause it's my show, my show
Don't know if people think I'm shallow,
shallow
But all I see is all eyes on me

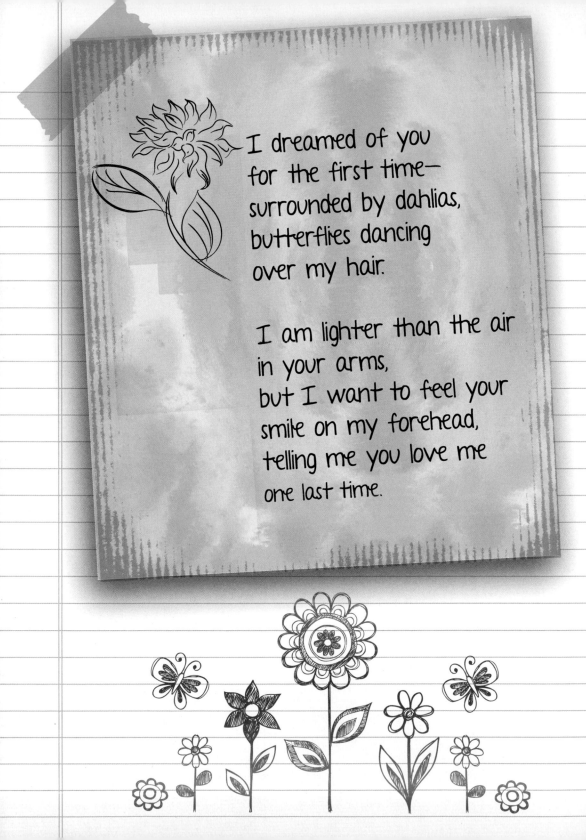

I dreamed of you
for the first time—
surrounded by dahlias,
butterflies dancing
over my hair.

I am lighter than the air
in your arms,
but I want to feel your
smile on my forehead,
telling me you love me
one last time.

Terms to Know in the 21st Century

Memes: It's kind of like a funny photo or video shared online with a relatable caption. For example: If I took a picture of you guys I'd write "Just got ghosted." *Even I know that's a lame joke.*

I think you'd be great at memes, Reggie.

Streaming: It's when you watch a video or listen to music online instead of downloading it.

Hits: It's basically how many people have seen or listened to something online. And the more hits your stuff gets, the better.

Woke: It's a way to describe someone who's on top of real-life issues and topics that are going on in the world.

So nothing to do with sleep, then.

Mood: When you see a picture of something—like, a cat hanging onto a tree branch—and it describes exactly how you feel on the inside, that's a mood.

Just when I thought being in a band with ghosts was complicated I get thrown into a dance battle for love. Today, I had my dance rehearsal with Nick! It was exactly like I used to daydream about. Everything between us felt easy and fun—and he kept making me laugh with his surprisingly inept dance moves. But still—I couldn't stop thinking about Luke.

It's just so crazy. I can't crush on a ghost! All the movies point to no for paranormal romance. But there's this weird, amazing, powerful connection between me and Luke that I just can't ignore. It's more than just chemistry; it's like we're two halves of the same song, and together we complete it.

And yeah, I know Flynn is right. I should stick with crushing
on the living—and I DO like Nick, too—but how can I stop what
I'm feeling for Luke? If I could bottle up these confusing feelings
and throw them into the ocean I would.

I don't think I can
keep doing this.

Julie! You finally have
a chance with Nick—who
is single, breathing, and
ALIVE, FYI—and you're just
going to throw it away
because of a GHOST?
You've written fan fiction
about dancing with Nick!

I know! And it was even
better than I could have
imagined. But I just couldn't
stop thinking about Luke.

You need to
come back
to the living
and focus
on what you
can actually
touch.

I know, Flynn.

Nick

- Cute
- Bad at dancing but in
  a charming way, like a
  puppy learning how
  to walk
- Really good at guitar
- Nice to everyone, but
  he can be a pushover
  because of it
- Great hair
- Athletic

Luke

- Perfect smile
- Super talented songwriter
- ALSO really good at guitar
- Cares about his friends
- Confident (to a fault)
- A good listener, even if he doesn't always know how to comfort you
- Sometimes gets tunnel vision and only thinks about music

What are you going to do when Luke figures out his unfinished business? I don't want you heartbroken about someone you can never have.

I don't know. I guess I'll cross that bridge when they cross over.

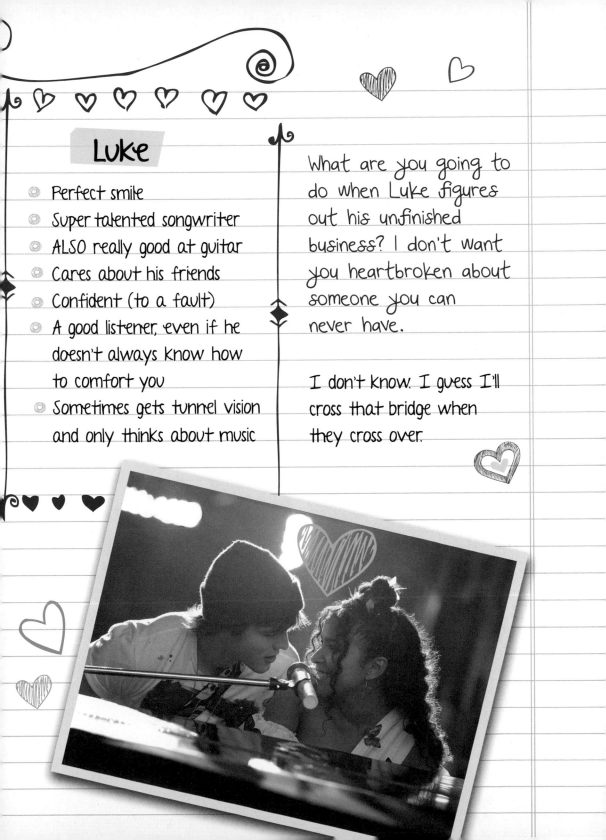

REPORT: **0024876944**
OPERATIVE: **C. MOLINA**

C L A S S I F I E D

Mission: █████████████████████

Objective: ████████████████████████████

Carlos's Ghost Log #15

I finally saw the ghosts in action, but I missed my chance at taking a photo! Stupid selfie mode!

To recap: I was looking for ghosts last night in the living room when, suddenly, the lights started going on and off and the curtains fluttered. Tía was with me, and she kept trying to logic her way through it, when all of a sudden these sheets started to float!

Floating sheets! The house <u>is</u> haunted! And I could've had proof, but the camera went off the wrong way, and then Tía dragged me out of the house.

Tía wanted us to move out that night or call a priest or something, but I told her, as the ghost expert of the house, I would handle it.

I think it's time to explore the final option for getting rid of ghosts. I need to figure out why they're still here—their unfinished business—so they can move on.

"Edge of Great"

Running from the past
Tripping on the now
What was lost can be found, it's obvious

And like a rubber ball
We come bouncing back
We all got a second act, inside of us

I believe
I believe
That we're just one dream
Away from who we're meant to be
That we're standing on the edge of

Something big, something crazy
Our best days are yet unknown
That this moment is ours to own
'Cause we're standing on the edge of

Great
On the edge of great
Great
On the edge of great
Great
On the edge of great

'Cause we're standing on the edge of
Great

We all make mistakes
But they're just stepping stones
To take us where we wanna go
It's never straight, no

Sometimes we gotta lean
Lean on someone else
To get a little help
Until we find our way

I believe
I believe
That we're just one dream
Away from who we're meant to be
That we're standing on the edge of

Something big, something crazy
Our best days are yet unknown
That this moment is ours to own
'Cause we're standing on the edge of

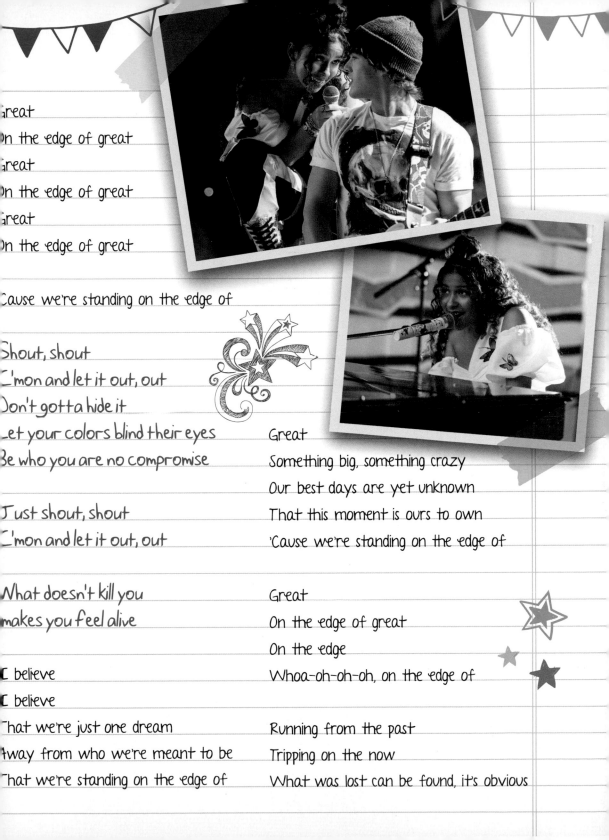

Great
On the edge of great
Great
On the edge of great
Great
On the edge of great

'Cause we're standing on the edge of

Shout, shout
C'mon and let it out, out
Don't gotta hide it
Let your colors blind their eyes
Be who you are no compromise

Just shout, shout
C'mon and let it out, out

Great
Something big, something crazy
Our best days are yet unknown
That this moment is ours to own
'Cause we're standing on the edge of

What doesn't kill you
makes you feel alive

Great
On the edge of great
On the edge
Whoa-oh-oh-oh, on the edge of

I believe
I believe
That we're just one dream
Away from who we're meant to be
That we're standing on the edge of

Running from the past
Tripping on the now
What was lost can be found, it's obvious

When Reggie, Alex, and I spied on Luke with his family, it reminded me how lost they really are. To the guys, it hasn't been twenty-five years since they died; it's only been a couple of weeks. I can't even imagine how it would feel if I woke up one day and saw Carlos all grown up, when just yesterday he was playing Little League.

Luke had wanted to make peace with his family before he died. He thought he could use his music to reach out to his mom and they could forgive each other. And the fact that his parents still celebrate his birthday after so many years shows that they wanted the same thing.

There must be something I can do to make this right for them. Luke helped so much as I've made peace with losing my mom. I just want to do the same for him.

Maybe . . . maybe it isn't too late for his song to be heard.

Do you ever miss your family like Luke does?

Not really. Things were never the same between me and my parents after I came out—especially with my dad. My parents avoided me all the time, and they wouldn't even look me in the eye. Just because I was gay. It got really lonely. It didn't really feel like home anymore.

I'm so sorry, Alex.

I mean, it sucked at the time, but I don't miss them as much as I thought I would. Luke and Reggie are all the family I need.

I get that. Sometimes family isn't the people you're born with but the ones you find.

Exactly.

And now you have Willie, too. ☺

Did Reggie tell you?

He likes to gossip! Don't be too hard on him.

Willie's great, we're just SO different. And he's been avoiding me lately . . . I don't know what's going on with us.

As someone who understands overcomplicating things, trust me that whatever's going on, it's probably not because of you. He'll talk to you when he's ready.

Thanks, Julie.

Alex's Rockin' Relaxation Playlist

♪ "Let There Be Rock"
by AC/DC

"Would That I"
by Hozier

"My Generation"
by the Who

"I Want to Hold Your Hand"
by the Beatles

"In the Air Tonight"
by Phil Collins

♪ "Rock and Roll"
by Led Zeppelin

"Electric Feel"
by MGMT

"Seven Nation Army"
by the White Stripes

"Dancing on My Own"
by Robyn

"Tell Me Something Good"
by Chaka Khan and Rufus

"Falling"
by Trevor Daniel

"Maniac"
♪ by Conan Gray

"Fool in the Rain"
by Led Zeppelin

So glad you liked some of the 21st-century stuff I recommended, Alex!
-J

"Unsaid Emily"

First things first
We start the scene in reverse
All of the lines rehearsed
Disappeared from my mind

When things got loud
One of us running out
I should have turned around
But I had too much pride

No time
For goodbyes
Didn't get to apologize
Pieces of a clock that lies broken

If I could take us back
If I could just do that
And write in every empty space
The words "I love you" in replace
Then maybe time would not erase me

If you could only know
I never let you go
And the words I most regret
Are the ones I never meant to leave
Unsaid Emily

Silent days
Mysteries and mistakes
Who'd be the first to break?
I guess we're alike that way

He said
She said
Conversations in my head
And that's just where
they're gonna stay
Forever

If I could take us back
If I could just do that
And write in every empty space
The words "I love you" in replace
Then maybe time would not erase me

If you could only know
I never let you go
And the words I most regret
Are the ones I never meant to leave
Unsaid Emily

If you could only know
I never let you go
And the words I most regret
Are the ones I never meant to leave
Unsaid Emily

If I could take us back
If I could just do that
And write in every empty space
The words "I love you" in replace
Then maybe time would not erase me

FLYNN'S FAVORITE
CONFIDENCE-BOOSTING BOPS

"How You Like That?" by BLACKPINK

"Do It" by Chloe x Halle

"Run the World (Girls)" by Beyoncé

"Grrrl Like" by Dope Saint Jude

"Suncity" by Khalid featuring Empress Of

"Material Girl" by Madonna

"Bad Guy" by Billie Eilish

"Si te vas" by Shakira

"Soy Yo" by Bomba Estéreo

"Boy with Luv" by BTS ft. Halsey

"Soulmate" by Lizzo

"Boys Will Be Boys" by Dua Lipa

"Rain on Me" by Lady Gaga and Ariana Grande

"Diva" by Beyoncé

"Tan Enamorados" by CNCO

"Fallin' (Adrenaline)" by Why Don't We

"De Una Vez" by Selena Gomez

RECIPE

Tía Victoria's
Famous Arroz con
Pollo Recipe

PREP TIME	COOK TIME	SERVING	DATE

DIRECTIONS

1. Season the chicken with adobo, o...
2. Cook the ch... ...per.
   off the ...
3. Lower ... ...heat until fully cooked. Take it
   of tor...
4. Add t...
5. Simmer...
6. Lower the ...
   cooked.

INGREDIENTS

...rs, olives, sazón, and half a can
...t a little. Then add the chicken.
...gone.
...t for fifteen minutes or until

¡Buen Provecho! And don't forget
to save a plate for your tía!

FROM THE KITCHEN OF

*Enjoy, mijos!
Call me if you
need help in the
kitchen!
—V*

From the Kitchen of _____

For _____

Flour   Sugar

Oh my gosh. So. Like, as much as I miss food, being a ghost is, like, pretty rad since I can, like, go anywhere I want.

What is this? Are you mocking me? I do NOT write like that.

And I also got to catch up on all the movies I missed, including the new Star Wars. Although, honestly, I would have been okay NOT seeing some of those. Watching a couple of them felt like when you drop a slice of pizza in the rain and can't afford another one.

But anyway, the best part is that sometimes the guys and I can bother Julie when she's in class, which she loves.

I do not love

Sure, she might throw an eraser or two at the window— and her teacher looks at her funny—but it's all right. *It isn't.*

But the really, really best part is that I get to hang out with Carlos and Ray whenever Julie's not home. They're cool people. It's like I'm their long-lost relative and we're just a couple of guys chilling out. Except I'm dead and one of them is a dad and the other keeps throwing salt everywhere whenever I put a blanket over my head. It's hilarious, though.

Dude. Why are you like this?

TOP SECRET

REPORT: **0024876944**

OPERATIVE: **C. MOLINA**

C L A S S I F I E D

Mission: ████████████████████

Objective: █████████████████████████

Carlos's Ghost Log #19

After digging around the studio, I found an old cardboard box up in the loft. It had a bunch of stuff in it. I figured it was some of Mom's old things. But then I found it. The ghost's unfinished business, their unfulfilled dream.

A recipe for the perfect French dip.

This has to be it! The missing piece I needed to help the ghost move on or cross over or whatever. If I can re-create their lost recipe, the ghost will finally leave us alone.

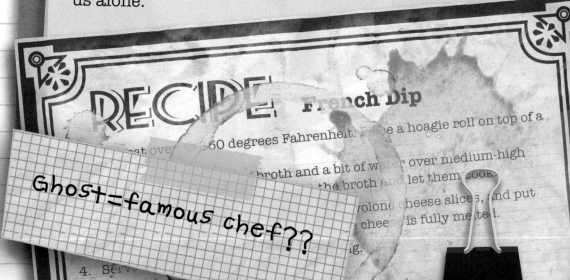

RECIPE French Dip

...at over... 50 degrees Fahrenheit. Place a hoagie roll on top of a

...broth and a bit of water over medium-high ...the broth and let them cook.

...rolone cheese slices, and put ...cheese is fully melted.

...g.

Ghost=famous chef??

4. Serv...

Some of my favorite memories of visiting family in Puerto Rico were the parties and festivals. Puerto Ricans will use any excuse to get together and make the party last as long as possible. That's why Carlos and I are so good at sleeping in chairs while the adults say goodbye for the fourth time in an hour.

One time, we drove down south to Ponce to see Carnaval, where everyone dresses up as vejigantes with these big colorful horned masks and capes. They danced the traditional bomba dance to celebrate Afro-Puerto Rican culture. The dance is like a conversation between the dancer, with their long billowing skirts, and the drummer, who beats to the dancer's movements. Even as a bystander, you feel the rhythm of the music move you.

Saludos desde Puerto Rico

Carnaval de Ponce

Puerto Rico

But the memories that stand out to me the most from every trip are the stories we'd hear. From the chupacabra and the gargoyle, to el cuco and even aliens! The folklore and superstition of the island stretches far and wide, and no story is ever told the same way twice. Sometimes these stories are told like a joke, but most of the time, they're told as a warning to always be careful of what's on the other side.

Letting go
is an exhale
after holding my breath
underwater for years.

Weightless, pressure hurting my lungs,
but I wish to hold it
for a little longer.

To inhale is to
let go of the now
as it becomes
back then.

Can I let go?
Or can I hold my breath
for just
a
little
longer?

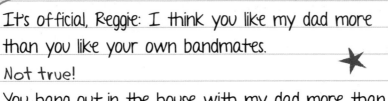

It's official, Reggie: I think you like my dad more than you like your own bandmates.

Not true!

You hang out in the house with my dad more than you hang out with Luke or Alex!

Listen, Ray is cool! And we have so much in common! Like how we both quote Star Wars all the time and can't understand cell phones.

Don't get me wrong—I'm glad you like him. But why do you like to keep him company so much? It's not like he can see you.

Spending time with him makes me miss my own parents a little less, you know? Plus, he's got a kind soul. And he's such a great dad. Ray listens to you! And he's always thinking about you and Carlos and making sure you're okay. He's a pretty awesome dad.

Yeah, he IS pretty awesome . . . Reggie, don't cry.

I am not crying. It's just ghost sweat.

Music has always been the heart of the Molina family. Mom used to say that it isn't just in our blood, it's in our culture, and the best way to connect with our roots is to listen to what our family would have listened to.

That helped me realize just how much we're influenced by what we listen to and how it can define our world.

For instance, my mom loved Menudo growing up, a Puerto Rican boy band from the '80s—Ricky Martin was in it when he was a kid! And she listened to the Runaways, the Beatles, David Bowie, and Carlos Ponce. Dad said he was really into Run DMC and Fleetwood Mac.

And they both grew up listening to Celia Cruz, el Gran Combo, and Héctor Lavoe—salsa and merengue were the background music of their lives growing up. It taught them to celebrate every little thing in life that's worth smiling for, and that to have fun, you just need good company to dance with.

BEHIND THE BAND:

An interview with the one-woman team behind Los Feliz's hottest new hologram band

SINCE JULIE and the Phantoms' first performance at the spirit rally, the band has become an overnight sensation—both in and out of school. Their first video, "Edge of Great"—filmed at the band's headquarters in Julie's garage—has over a half million views after just two days. And with the way things are going, the sky's the limit. We've got an exclusive interview with the band's social media manager, Flynn Taylor, who's been behind the scenes since day one.

LOS FELIZ HIGH: Flynn, you and Julie are longtime friends. She even wrote a song just for you! How do you feel about Julie's success?

FLYNN: We've been inseparable since we were six, and we've been each other's cheerleaders and number one fans from the start. I'm proud my bestie is getting the recognition she deserves.

Claw Times

Volume 10, Issue 15

LOS FELIZ HIGH: How did you become the band's social media manager?

LYNN: As someone who already has several accounts dedicated to my many hobbies— fashion, food, movies, music— what's handling a few more? I was the natural choice.

LOS FELIZ HIGH: Let's talk origin stories. Julie and the Phantoms isn't Julie's first band. How did Double Trouble come to be?

LYNN: I can't believe you know about that! Since we were kids, we wanted to be a rock and hip-hop showstopper. Teaming up came naturally.

LOS FELIZ HIGH: Is there a chance for a Double Trouble and Julie and the Phantoms collab?

LYNN: We shall see!

LOS FELIZ HIGH: Anything you can tell us about those hunky holograms? Who are the guys behind the technology?

LYNN: Oh, uh, well, I can't really talk much about them. They want to keep their identities a secret. People love a good mystery, amirite?

"Perfect Harmony"

Step into my world
Bittersweet love story about a girl

Shook me to the core
Voice like an angel
I've never heard before

Here in front of me
Shining so much brighter
Than I have ever seen

Life can be so mean
But when he goes
I know he doesn't leave

The truth is finally breaking through
Two worlds collide when I'm with you
Our voices rise and soar so high

We come to life when we're
In perfect harmony

Whoa whoa
Perfect harmony
Whoa whoa
Perfect harmony

You set me free
You and me together is more
than chemistry
Love me as I am
I'll hold your music here inside
my hands

We say we're friends
We play pretend

You're more to me, we're
everything

Our voices rise and soar so high
We come to life when we're
In perfect harmony

Whoa whoa
Perfect harmony
Whoa whoa
Perfect harmony

I feel your rhythm in my heart
Yeah

You are my brightest, burning star
Whoa

I never knew a love so real
So real

Whoa whoa
Perfect harmony
Whoa whoa

We're heaven on earth
Melody and words
When we are together we're
In perfect harmony

We say we're friends
We play pretend

You're more to me

We create
Perfect harmony

Possible Unfinished Business

- Eat a slice of pizza at every single pizzeria in LA

- Eat a taco from every taco place in LA

- Make peace with family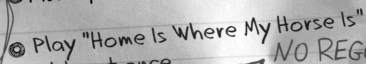

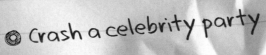
Been there, done that

Hard pass

Ditto

- Play "Home Is Where My Horse Is" at least once 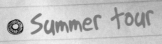 NO REGGIE

- Summer tour

- Crash a celebrity party

- Go platinum

- Win a Grammy

- Play the Orpheum

Reggie's Guilty Pleasure Playlist

"9 to 5" by Dolly Parton

"Take on Me" by a-ha

"I'd Do Anything for Love (But I Won't Do That)" by Meat Loaf

"Uptown Girl" by Billy Joel

"Don't You (Forget About Me)" by Simple Minds

"Jolene" by Dolly Parton

"Old Town Road" by Lil Nas X ft. Billy Ray Cyrus

"Achy Breaky Heart" by Billy Ray Cyrus

"You Belong with Me" by Taylor Swift

"Grandma's Hands" by Willie Nelson ft. Mavis Staples

"Dead of Night" by Orville Peck

"What Makes You Beautiful" by One Direction

"Take It Easy" by the Eagles

"Twist and Shout" by the Beatles

How did you even find out about some of these songs?

Carlos leaves his laptop open sometimes.

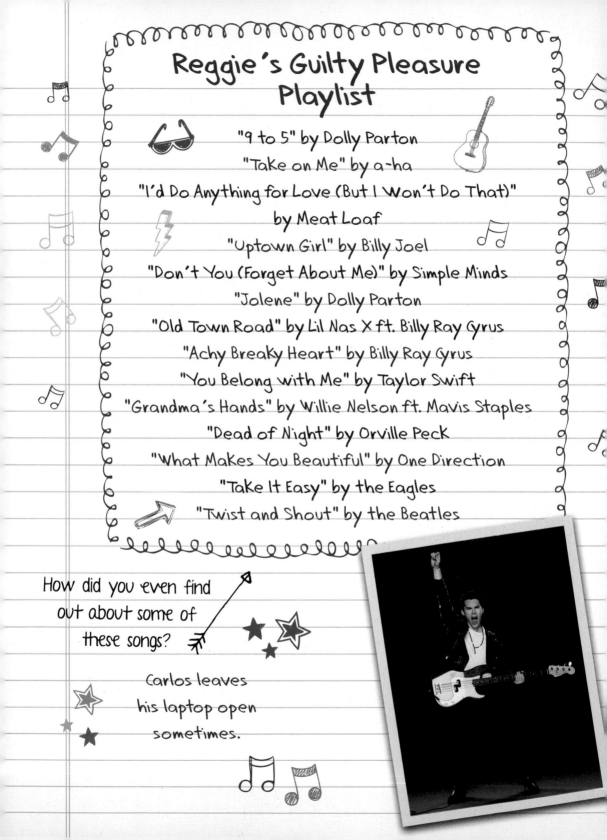

Playing the Orpheum, Take 2

1. Find out the name of the band opening for Panic! At The Disco

   We can use Julie's phone for this—technology!

2. Track down their location

3. Get Willie to find their tour bus

4. Willie will somehow drive the bus to get them as far away from LA as possible

5. Poof into the booking agent's office and play our video at the perfect moment

   Ghost powers GOOOO!!!

6. Get them Julie's phone number

   I'll handle the writing this time, so we can avoid another "Julie and the Phat Ones" situation

   That was one time!

I don't have a lot of time to write this before Caleb forces us back onstage. (Can ghosts suffer from burnout?)

I can't believe Caleb trapped us here. I knew that we had accidentally signed our souls away to the club, but I had no idea he'd go as far as to actually kidnap us!

We're supposed to be at the Orpheum right now. Julie is probably freaking out. I promised myself I would never let Julie down again. Disappointing her and nearly losing her trust was the worst feeling in the world—and I've DIED.

Not to mention how much she did to help me and my family find peace again before I cross over... I owe her this.

But now... after we finally got our chance to play the Orpheum, Caleb snatched us away. And just like that, our second chance is gone, just like last time.

There has to be some way to get out of this. Some sort of sign would be great...

SET LIST
ORPHEUM THEATRE

"STAND TALL"

"BRIGHT"

"FINALLY FREE"

"FLYING SOLO"

"EDGE OF GREAT"

A woman found me crying
alone in the streets
as I begged for a sign,
a word,
a music note—
anything to prove
that you're still with me.

The woman,
a stranger,
carrying her groceries down the
streets of angels,
smiled and gave me a flower.
A dahlia.
Your favorite.
Is this your answer?

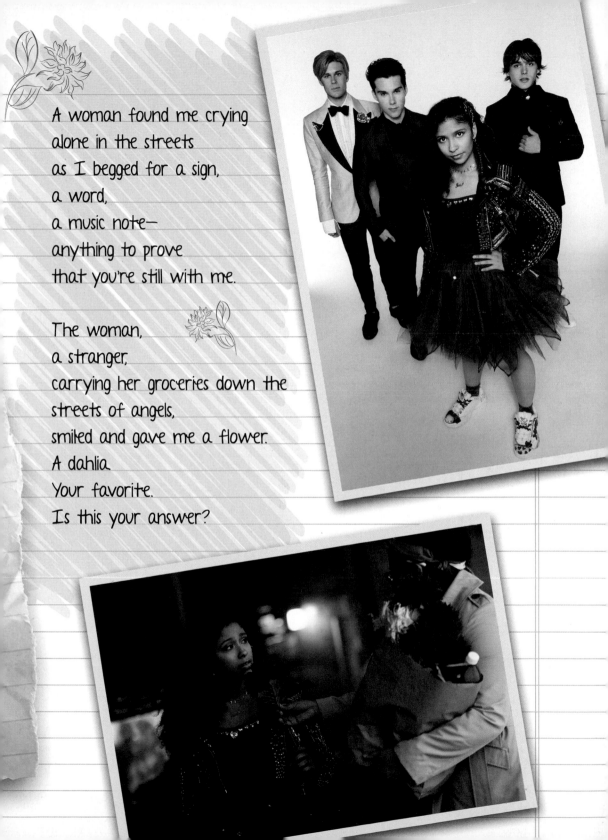

"Stand Tall"

Don't blink
No, I don't want to miss it
One thing
And it's back to the beginning
'Cause everything is rushing in fast
Keep going on never look back

And it's one, two, three, four times
That I'll try for one more night
Light a fire in my eyes
I'm going out of my mind

Whatever happens
Even if I'm the last standing
I'mma stand tall
I'mma stand tall

Whatever happens
Even when everything's down
I'mma stand tall
I'mma stand tall

I gotta keep on dreaming
'Cause I gotta catch that feeling
Whatever happens
Even if I'm the last standing
I'mma stand tall
I'mma stand tall

Right now
I'm loving every minute
Hands down
Can't let myself forget it, no
'Cause everything is rushing in fast
Keep holding on never look back

And it's one, two, three, four time
That I'll try for one more night
Light a fire in my eyes

I'm going out of my mind
Whatever happens
Even if I'm the last standing
I'mma stand tall
I'mma stand tall

Whatever happens
Even when everything's down
I'mma stand tall
I'mma stand tall

I gotta keep on dreaming
'Cause I gotta catch that feeling

Whatever happens
Even if I'm the last standing
I'mma stand tall
I'mma stand tall

Like I'm glowing in the dark
I keep on going when it's all falling apart
Yeah, I know with all my heart
Ooo, ooo
Never look back

Whatever happens
Even if I'm the last standing
I'mma stand tall
I'mma stand tall

Whatever happens
Even if I'm the last standing
I'mma stand tall
I'mma stand tall

Stand tall
Stand tall

Whatever happens
Even if I'm the last standing
I'mma stand tall
I'mma stand tall

Whatever happens
Even when everything's down
I'mma stand tall
I'mma stand tall

I gotta keep on dreaming
'Cause I gotta catch that feeling

Whatever happens
Even if I'm the last standing
I'mma stand tall
I'mma stand tall

When I heard that the band opening for Panic! At The Disco at their Orpheum show this past weekend hasn't even released a single I was, admittedly, a little skeptical. But after watching them play live, I understand why so many people call their music *haunting*.

The local band was added to the lineup at the last minute when Panic!'s original openers, Downslide, encountered some travel issue cn route to the venue. (Downslide's manager declined to comment for this story.)

Their replacement, Julie and the Phantoms, is a hologram band (with the exception of their lead singer, the eponymous Julie Molina). Their first video, "Edge of Great," was uploaded less than three days ago and has already racked up nearly a million views, a number I'm sure has skyrocketed after their Orpheum debut.

Their set was like falling in love with rock and roll all over again. It reminded me of days spent driving down the West Coast with your closest friends and shouting the lyrics of your favorite songs out of the windows. Their music is a love song to the greats who paved the way for novice rockers like them.

Julie and the Phantoms' opening song, "Stand Tall," is Journey's "Don't Stop Believin'" meets Queen's "Under Pressure": a reminder to fight for what you want, regardless of the obstacles in your way. Following that were "Bright," "Finally Free," and "Flying Solo." The band finished their set of original songs—a true feat at this stage of their career—with "Edge of Great," proving to this reviewer that Julie and the Phantoms will not be a one-hit wonder.

So get ready, world; here they come.

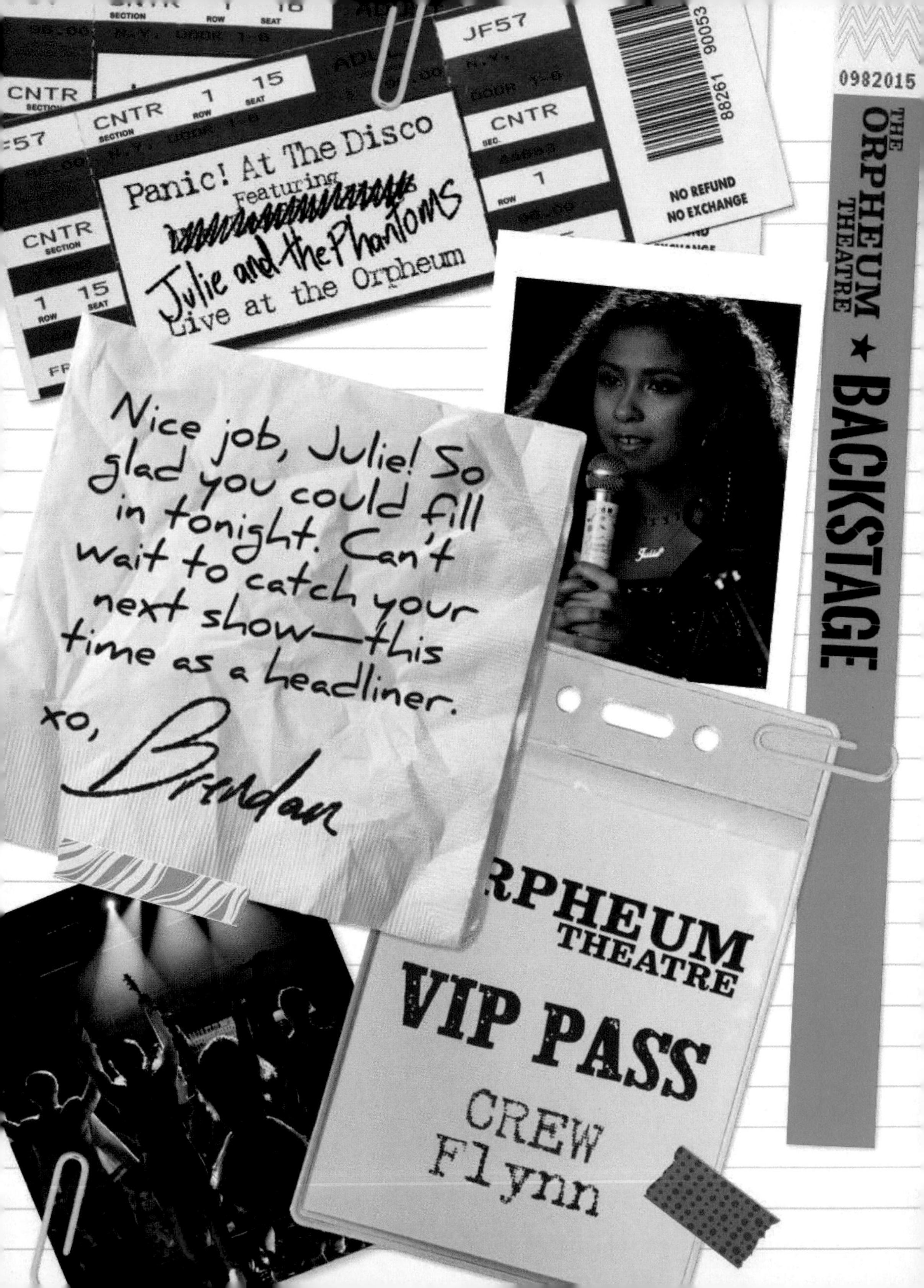

Panic! At The Disco
Featuring ~~~~~~~~~~
Julie and the Phantoms
Live at the Orpheum

CNTR SECTION
ROW 1 SEAT 15
ADULT N.Y. DOOR 1-6
JF57
CNTR
88261 90053
NO REFUND
NO EXCHANGE

THE ORPHEUM THEATRE ★ BACKSTAGE
0982015

Nice job, Julie! So glad you could fill in tonight. Can't wait to catch your next show—this time as a headliner.

xo,
Brendan

ORPHEUM THEATRE
VIP PASS
CREW
Flynn

Julie and the Phantoms lives! Not literally, because 3/4 of your members are still dead—sort of, I guess? Whatever, we need to start thinking big. I'm thinking groupies. I'm thinking touring. I'm thinking merchandise.

How many sodas did you drink backstage?

At least six, but that's not the point! The point is that the Orpheum was just the first step—a big step!—and now it's time to spread the awesomeness of JATP. I'm thinking we start with some merch, get a demo, some shirts . . .

We should post another video soon, too!

Yes! Then we can do a summer tour! I'm thinking Coachella, followed up with a few other summer fests. Do a cross-country road trip hitting the big music cities—I'm thinking Austin, Nashville, then wrap things up in New York!

How about we pass our final exams first before getting in the van?

Ugh, if we must.

I was so tired from the roller coaster that was yesterday I almost crashed as soon as we got home. From excitement to fear, anger to hopelessness, sadness to joy ... I don't think there's a single song that could describe it all.

The show was AMAZING. I got so many business cards from so many managers, and my wrists hurt from signing so many autographs. I even heard that someone wrote an article about us!

And if that wasn't enough, to cap off the night, I actually hugged the guys. Like, actually, physically hugged them! I don't know how or why, but once we touched, the Ghost Club brands on their arms floated away.

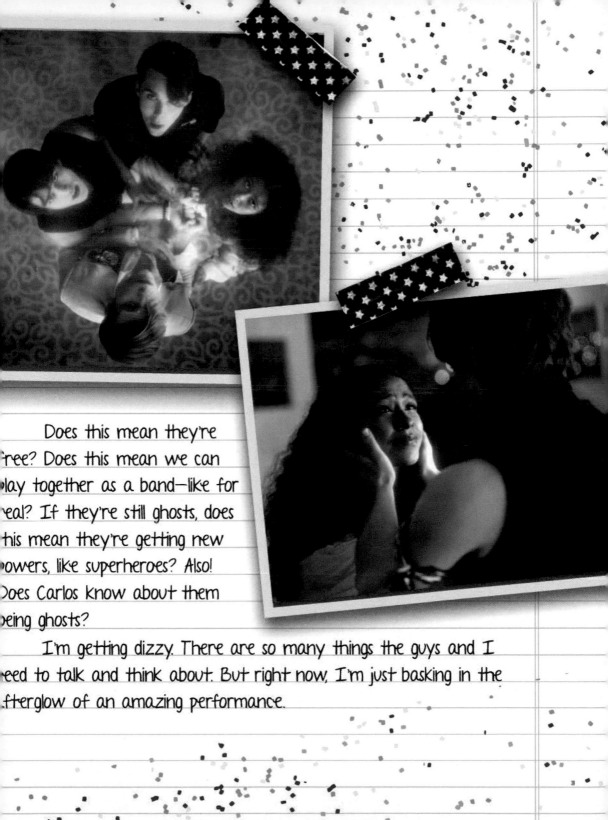

Does this mean they're free? Does this mean we can play together as a band—like for real? If they're still ghosts, does this mean they're getting new powers, like superheroes? Also! Does Carlos know about them being ghosts?

I'm getting dizzy. There are so many things the guys and I need to talk and think about. But right now, I'm just basking in the afterglow of an amazing performance.

As much as I love being able to hug Julie, shouldn't we think about WHY she can feel us when we're still technically ghosts?

Well, yeah, but I can't think of anything that explains it.

Maybe we're getting more powerful? Like, with the power of love—or music!

That's sweet, but I don't think so.

I think we should be more worried about Caleb. There's no way he's going to just let us go, right?

Yeah, the guy already can't take no for an answer. I don't want to picture him when he loses what he wants.

I'm more worried about Willie. What if Caleb finds out he helped us?

Willie's smart. He's been around longer than we have. He'll figure it out.

Do you think we can eat pizza now?

Nothing fazes you, huh, Reg?

Mission: ████████████████████

Objective: ████████████████████

Carlos's Ghost Log #22

I knew it, I knew it, I knew it! There <u>are</u> ghosts haunting our house—and they're Julie's bandmates! My sister talks to ghosts! I thought she was being super weird lately, but it all makes sense now. Holograms? Who even does that anymore?

This was better than any <u>Ghost Hunters</u> episode ever, and I had to get proof.

But when I went to Mom's studio to record the evidence, I overheard Julie talking to one of them . . . Luke, I think. They were talking about him crossing over. She asked him to find Mom and thank her for bringing the band to Julie and getting her back into music.

I deleted the video. I had to. If these ghosts helped my sister, and if Mom brought them to her, I shouldn't post that online. This has to stay in the family.

I tease my sister a lot, but I love her too much. (But I would never say that to her face. Ever.) And I'm really happy she's back to her weird self again. A year without

her music was like a desert with no water, or a weekend without pizza, or Tía's arroz con pollo without tembleque for dessert.

So if these guys are good for her, they're okay in my book. Case closed.

If I had to pick a color to describe the year after losing Mom, I'd say it was gray. And the music I tried to listen to sounded just as muted and dull. Some days, the gray was so bad I couldn't get out of bed or eat or do anything.

My therapist, Dr. Turner, told me it was important to take the gray one day at a time. And whenever there was a burst of color—a good song on the radio, delicious food, something that made me laugh—I should write it down to remember the feeling. Things wouldn't magically get better, but they would get easier with time.

She was right. I did get bursts of color thanks to my friends and family. And even though I couldn't play music, listening to it helped. It wasn't always easy, but I had the best support system in the world, and that made the gray days a little more bearable.

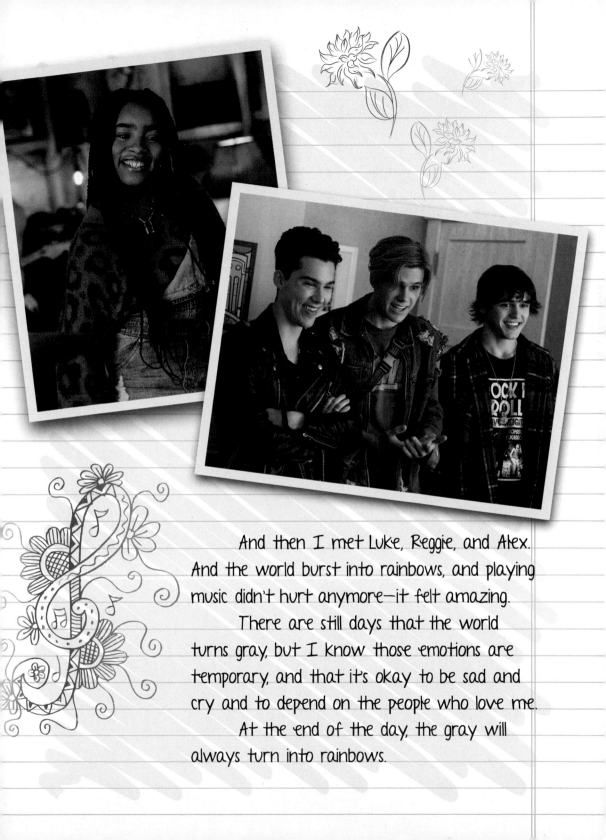

And then I met Luke, Reggie, and Alex. And the world burst into rainbows, and playing music didn't hurt anymore—it felt amazing.

There are still days that the world turns gray, but I know those emotions are temporary, and that it's okay to be sad and cry and to depend on the people who love me.

At the end of the day, the gray will always turn into rainbows.

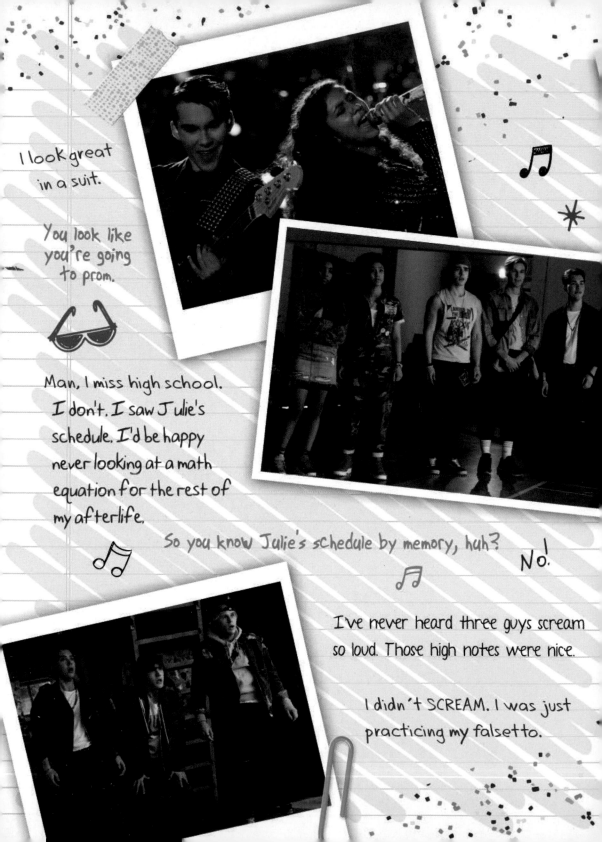

I look great in a suit.

You look like you're going to prom.

Man, I miss high school. I don't. I saw Julie's schedule. I'd be happy never looking at a math equation for the rest of my afterlife.

So you know Julie's schedule by memory, huh?

No!

I've never heard three guys scream so loud. Those high notes were nice.

I didn't SCREAM. I was just practicing my falsetto.

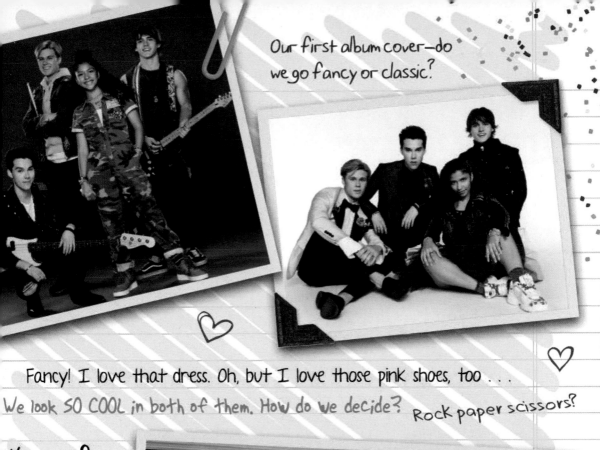

Our first album cover—do
we go fancy or classic?

Fancy! I love that dress. Oh, but I love those pink shoes, too . . .
We look SO COOL in both of them. How do we decide? Rock paper scissors?

I had the worst wedgie that entire song.
Dude . . . we don't need to know about your ghost wedgies.

Angel Face,

If I could write all the things I wanted to teach you as you grow up into this letter I would. If I could save up all my hugs for the firsts in your life: your first kiss, your first heartbreak, your first Grammy, or even just a hug because you miss me, I'd bottle them up and tell you to save them for a rainy day.

But I'm not worried. I know you will grow up to be great, because you already are. You will grow and flourish with your music, and you will change the world, just like you changed mine when I held you in my arms for the very first time.

I know you will be sad. I know you're worried about your papá and your brother. But you have each other, and you always will.

And if you ever miss me, Angel Face, sing for me. I'll always be listening.

Look for me in the dahlias.

Con todo mi corazón,

Tu mamá